AGENT RED:FATAL ENEMY

TEAGAN STONE BOOK 5

AVA S. KING

304 PUBLISHING COMPANY

INTRODUCTION

Sign-up to Ava S. King's mailing list for news, new releases and special offers.

https://landing.mailerlite.com/webforms/landing/r7j2s6

*I want to dedicate this book to my family and friends.
You are always with me, no matter where I go, and
everything you've taught me has made me a better person.*

DISCLAIMER

This work of fiction contains strong language and explicit content and is only intended for mature readers. This story may contain unconventional situations, language, and sexual encounters that may offend some readers. This book is for mature readers (18+).

SYNOPSIS

Enemies come in all forms, and Teagan Stone is ready for battle, not thinking of the consequences for going to war with her ultimate rival. Can she turn back the clock or will this lead her to finally leave The Firm before it destroys her from within?

LATEST RELEASES:AVA S. KING

Agent Red:Fatal Memory Teagan Stone Book 1
Agent Red:Fatal Target Teagan Stone Book 2
Agent Red:Fatal Crime Teagan Stone Book 3
Agent Red:Fatal Justice Teagan Stone Book 4
Agent Red:Fatal Enemy Teagan Stone Book 5
Upcoming Releases (2022/2023)
Mirror of Lies -A Jessica Smith Book 1
Agent Red: Fatal Death Teagan Stone Book 6
Agent Red: Fatal Revenge Teagan Stone Book 7
Mirror of Lust -A Jessica Smith Book 2
Chris Harris Mystery/Thriller Series

ONE

Camden, Nebraska small town.

Teagan stood back in the stalky, narrow grass at the uncovered buried bodies of five victims, some as young as thirteen up to twenty-three years old. Closing her eyes for a moment, she took in the chill of the Maryland weather. Having to get a call in the middle of the night from her team about a police tip about women being buried out here wasn't on her agenda for today. As she stood with her arms crossed and listening to birds chirping, police tried to block reporters from contaminating the evidence. Teagan only wanted to have a second to herself. In her mind, this could be her daughter Tatum. Having to contact the parents of these missing girls would undoubtedly hurt, but this came with the lifestyle. Even before she arrived, word spread up to Congress and the White House that a serial killer was on the loose. So before she could decline to take the case, the president made her aware that this was the reason The Firm was created. To handle certain things that local police wouldn't be able to unload promptly.

"What are your thoughts?" Teagan's eyes popped open at the sound of his voice.

"Human trafficking," they answered at the same time, clogging through the tall field of weeds that almost hit her knees. From the signs on the road at the entrance of the field, this place had been abandoned for some time—nothing for miles.

Spider could tell she was taking this case personally, and there was no use in trying to push it off on the FBI to oversee. The sun was starting to set as the crime scene photographer finished, allowing the coroner to load the body bags. Stepping closer, Teagan glanced around the area, sensing it was probably disrupted by reporters or police.

"Who was the officer that got the call?" Teagan questioned.

"The guy that's talking to the reporters right now." Spider pointed at a group of people standing off at the far end of the field.

Teagan turned her head to the right and glanced at Officer Peter Copeland smiling in front of the camera like he was the hero.

"Get those reporters out of here, and I want to know why this happened," Teagan stated, taking a minute to digest what was in front of her. The crime scene was taped off, but she'd bet the media would have photos out before she even got the girls' names to confirm with family.

"Teagan, you know as well as I do that this is going to be too much for you."

Teagan squatted down, staring at the outlines of the shallow graves; each body was laid out with their eyes closed and marks on their arms and legs from either being dragged or beaten in some form.

"I'm fine; I can handle myself." Teagan sighed, standing and removing the rubber gloves from her hands. Turning, she headed back to the car where Sean held open the door for her.

"Gather up as much information and send it to my office."

"Are we staying in town?" Spider asked.

Teagan glanced at the surrounding area, seeing the news reporters and police trying to block residents from coming near the crime scene.

"We'll see where the evidence leads us."

Closing the door behind her, Teagan removed her vibrating cell phone from her pocket, noticing Christian texting to check in on her trip.

Christian: I saw the news.

Teagan sighed, annoyed at the media already putting out the story.

Teagan: Kiss the kids for me.

Christian: How long will you be there?

Teagan: Not sure; I'll call you once I get back to the hotel.

Christian: I love you.

Teagan: I love you more.

Sliding her cell back in her jacket pocket, Teagan bit her bottom lip, thinking about the young girls and women that were found. Finding them like this only brought out the anxiety of her daughter being in a situation like those girls and not having anyone to protect them.

"Hotel, boss?" Sean asked.

"Take me to the mayor's office," Teagan answered.

Sean pressed the gas of the black, tinted, government-assigned SUV, turning out of the grassy farm area, and getting back on the main street. It was now going on three years since the Maksim case, and she was more ingrained in her role as director of The Firm. All the kids were getting older and wanting to be with their friends, but as their mom, she had to keep the socializing to a minimum. President Sanders was no longer at the helm of the government agency; the department of defense now managed it. After Duncan took his own life, President Sanders wanted to keep any individual from Congress from being able to cause another terrorist attack. So Teagan and her team reported to Pentagon headquarters while still having a single branch office in New York to work out of on a day-to-day basis. The car arrived in front of the mayor's office. Sean started to get out and open the door, but Teagan held her hand up, letting him know she was fine.

"I won't be long." Teagan looked up at the building, checking the time on her watch. Heading inside, she walked up to the reception desk.

"Hello. Can I help you?" the brunette with a short bob asked.

"I need to speak with the mayor."

"You are?" she questioned, scanning Teagan up and down.

Teagan stared at her nameplate on the desk, picking it up and repeating the name to herself.

"Audrey?"

"Yes."

"I'm Agent Stone, the person who was flown out here to solve the murder of young girls."

Audrey's mouth opened and closed, eyes blinked in surprise at her statement.

"Uhm, the mayor's available to speak now."

"I thought so."

Teagan placed the nameplate back on her desk and headed to the open door of Mayor Lloyd Henton. Knocking on the door, the mayor sat up in his seat, turning off the TV and fixing his tie.

"Am I interrupting you?" Teagan pointed toward the chair in front of his desk, and he stood, motioning to have a seat.

"You're the agent from the news." Lloyd grabbed his coat off the back of his chair, buttoning it up. He was about five feet ten with a receding hairline, black buzz cut, round belly, and a scar above his lip.

"You're the mayor."

Clearing his throat, they passed a look between each other, and Lloyd waited for Teagan to speak. Lloyd's been at the job for a year after his father retired and helped him to win the votes of the community. Lloyd was only in it to gain notoriety and sleep with women. At thirty-eight, his life growing up as the son of Bert and Amy Henton wasn't always good. He was never seen as the popular guy in school.

"I need to have full cooperation from your police department."

"That's fine; I don't see that being an issue."

"As you know, whenever outside authority comes in, some jurisdictions feel left out."

"I can assure you my office will give you the utmost support," Lloyd said, stretching his hand out for a shake.

Teagan looked at his hand and back up to his eyes, and he turned to start typing on his computer.

"Will your team need any accommodations?"

"We have a hotel for now."

Right as he started to answer, Audrey knocked on the door and stepped inside with some papers in her hand.

"Sir, the latest job numbers came through." Audrey placed the documents on his desk.

Teagan watched Audrey as she stepped near Lloyd, pointing at the pile of paperwork with her hand on the back of his chair. Studying her movements and seeing the ring on her finger, she assumed they were possibly very intimate with each other.

"How long have you been mayor, Mr. Henton?" They fell into silence as Audrey reached down, leaving the messages on top of his desk and walking out of his office.

"About a little over a year. My father retired, so I took his place."

She didn't know what to expect from him, but she could tell Llyod wasn't as confident in himself; keeping the police intact would be a bigger job if Llyod couldn't even handle keeping his secretary from giving them away. Rising out of her seat Teagan prepared to leave his office.

"I'll be in touch; if anything else comes up, please call me." Teagan left the card of the hotel she was staying at on his desk, turned, and left him to ponder what's about to happen in his city now that dead bodies of young girls are being found. Holding the door open, Teagan gets in the back passenger side as Sean steps around and climbs in on the driver's side, turning the key in the ignition and driving back to the Hilton Hotel. Her phone rings, and she notices Gregory calling.

"I'm on my way to the hotel now," Teagan said.

"We might have a problem," Gregory replied.

She groaned, throwing her head back in frustration, not having the patience to deal with a problem so early on.

"What's the problem?"

"The police chief won't release any records to me."

"Are you sure?"

"Yeah, I've been going back and forth with him on the phone."

Letting out a frustrated breath, Teagan scratches the back of her neck, wondering if it's going to be one of those missions with the local police thinking big government agents are coming in on their territory. Limiting interference from local agencies has helped to keep leaks from getting into the press. If Teagan needed to play a little hardball, she was up to the challenge. They were learning not only about this case but also having to serve under the Pentagon and Sanders no longer as a go-to contact. The Agency will have to be strategic with how they handle themselves going forward without causing a bigger public outcry.

"Send me his name."

TWO

The room was filled with local drunks, petty college boys, and a few men in suits that looked like they were on the brink of tears. Teagan half expected the local police station wouldn't be so full of criminals and busy with phones ringing off the hook. Pushing through the crowd, she stood at the front counter behind an older lady speaking with the Officer about her cat getting kidnapped.

"I need someone to come by and search," the older woman suggested.

"Miss Alma, we already told you your cat died a year ago," Officer replied, rolling his eyes.

"Now, young man, I pay your salary," Alma said, waving her hand around the room.

"We'll get someone out to your house soon," the Policeman said, motioning for Teagan to step forward.

"Good," Alma responded, smiling, showing off her missing tooth in the front row.

Leaving, she bumped into Teagan and almost fell.

"Ooh, sorry, young lady."

Teagan held her up as a young man rushed in and grabbed hold of her.

"Auntie, how many times do I have to tell you about running off!"

"Leave me alone, Bert!" Alma fussed, pushing Bert's hand away.

Everyone minded their business, not paying them any attention, and Teagan was shocked at Bert's aggressive approach.

"That's it; you're going into a nursing home," Bert said.

Alma shook her head, walking off as he followed behind, yelling at her back.

"Can I help you?"

"Uh, is someone going to help her?" Teagan asked, pointing at the door Alma walked out of with Bert.

"That's Alma for you. Bert can handle her."

"His approach seems a little unorthodox."

"Again, what can I help you with?"

Sensing her patience was about to be tested, Teagan cocked her neck left, then right.

"I need to speak with the captain."

"Why?"

"Classified."

He chuckled at her response.

"Lady, I don't know who you think you are—"

Teagan held up her ID showing a government agency, cutting him off.

"I can be your friend or your worst nightmare. What would you like, Edwin?" Teagan tapped his name badge and smirked.

"Hold on, let me check if he's available."

"Make him available."

Edwin scowled, stomping to the back while Teagan

stared looked around the station at the chaos and lack of structure inside. A second later, Edwin came back and told her to follow him to the Chief's office. All the men turned their heads, staring at the woman in all black and hair pulled into a ponytail wearing a turtleneck and black jeans, and leather boots. Her plan was to go straight to the hotel and wrap up the case, eat a late lunch, and call her kids. But somehow, things never go as expected in her day. Edwin pushed the door open, and she stepped inside as the captain motioned for her to take a seat as he talked on the phone.

"Personally, I think you should go back to Washington," Chief Barrett said, hanging up the phone and leaning back in his chair, holding eye contact with her. Keeping her gaze, so there was no doubt she wasn't to be intimated. Teagan's gone to war and back, kidnapped, and tortured. A small-town Chief with an ego that's probably bigger than what he has between his pants isn't going to deter her. She crossed her hands, glanced at the photos hanging on the wall.

"Chief Barrett, I see you have a beautiful family."

"Call me Sylvester."

"Call me Teagan."

"I didn't ask for you to be here; my men can handle this case."

Teagan whistled, clasping her hands together.

"You don't believe that."

"Watch your mouth and show some respect."

"That goes two ways, Sylvester. You want us gone, and I want to find the person that did this."

"Who do you think you are!"

"You're going to get on that phone and give my men whatever they need."

"And if I don't?" His nose flared, and his brows dipped low.

"Then you'll find out who I really am and how high my name runs in Washington."

Standing, Teagan turned, heading toward the door, and pushed the photo hanging on the wall to the left by an inch to straighten it out as she left out of his office.

"Looks much better now, don't you think," she said, smiling.

———

GREGORY SAT ACROSS FROM SPIDER, Daughtry, and Teagan at the local diner three blocks from the hotel. Broderick was outside on the phone with the coroner's office as they sat huddled together eating and debriefing about the day.

"This burger is probably the best thing I've had all day," Daughtrey mentioned, taking another bite of the double cheeseburger, popping fries in his mouth. Right as they landed at the airport, it was straight to the scene without eating a proper meal. Spider reached over to steal a fry off his plate.

"Get your own man," Daughtrey scoffed, trying to move his plate out of the way.

"Boys, please."

Spider smacked the back of his head.

"Chief Barrett sent over the information." Gregory drank his Coke, wiping his mouth on the napkin.

"Did he say anything?"

"Basically, if we screw up, it's on us," Gregory grunted, taking a slice of his pizza.

"He's not happy we're here."

"You don't say." Spider sighed, running a hand across his forehead.

The waitress came back with another plate of fries and cheeseburger, setting it in front of Daughtrey.

"Here you are, sweetheart." The older woman tapped Daughtrey on the shoulder, going back to the employee kitchen.

"Your arteries are going to be clogged for a while."

"What did I miss?" Broderick spoke, coming back to the table, sitting next to Spider.

"What did they say?" Teagan asked.

"He's emailing over the findings by tomorrow."

"Stay on top of him; we can't let them hinder us from solving this crime."

"How did it go with the mayor?" Spider inquired.

"He's more open to helping us; the Chief will need a little push."

"How long do we have to be here?" Daughtrey questioned.

"Shouldn't be more than a few days, open and closed case."

"I still can't believe those girls were killed and left like that." Spider drifted off in thought.

"I can," Teagan replied; all the guys looked oddly at her.

"You know I never publicly apologized in front of the guys," Broderick started to say.

She peered at him.

"Me too. I know we talked in passing, but we got in over our head Teagan," Daughtrey explained.

"Change the subject and talk about what we know so far." Teagan took charge, getting everyone's attention. Agreeing, they listened to her breakdown what they know so far from each one laid in a specific pose with bruises on their body. Pulling out a map of the area, Teagan marked the spots where their bodies were found, along with the photos from the scene that were sent over. Hoping to give them some closure is a promise she wants to keep so they can rest in peace.

LYING in bed with the tv playing, Teagan listened to Tatum talk about her day as she rambled on about how her brothers were getting on her nerves. She wanted to laugh but decided not to interrupt her and look like she was taking their sides.

"Mommy, you have to hurry home," Tatum demanded.

"That's the plan sweetheart, is your Daddy there?"

"Hm... uhh."

"Can I talk to him?"

"Is that Mom?" Teagan heard CJ ask.

"Yes, and she wants to talk to Daddy," Tatum spat.

"Let me see the phone," CJ spoke.

"No!" she heard a rustling over the phone.

"All right, you two, get ready for bed," Christian said; Teagan lowered the volume on the TV, pulling the comforter over her waist.

"Hi."

"Hi."

"I take it; you've made it back to the hotel."

Staring at the screen of a rerun from the housewives reality show, Teagan lifted the remote and changed the channel to something that would help her sleep. Normally she'd have Christian in bed, but not having him to hold and snuggle up against, she figured a movie would help.

"We did. How was your day?"

"Long but rewarding."

"How so?"

"I signed a few clients."

"That's amazing, baby."

"Thanks and the kids had their usual activities."

"I should be home soon." She turned to her side.

"My wife is the big-time agent; I saw the news."

"They showed me on the news?"

"Yeah, showing a possible serial killer."

"I told them to not let reporters get close to the scene."

"Too late, they had your name and where you work."

"Are the kids okay?"

"A few reporters called the house, but I hung up. After the bombing situation, you're more famous, babe."

"Not something I'm looking forward to being."

"I guess I should let you get some sleep."

"No, stay on the phone. I sleep better with you next to me."

Christian chuckled on the other end of the call. It was getting later and later as her eyes grew drowsy as she listened to Christian moving around the room.

"Just be safe."

Hearing the water turn on in the bathroom, Teagan thought it was time to get off the phone, so he could relax and get some sleep since he had to get up with the kids in the morning.

"Hey."

"Yeah, honey?"

"Have a good night. I'm going to let you go."

"You sure?"

"Yes, I love you."

"I love you more."

They listened to each other breathing for a few moments, hearing the silence echo across the lingering doubts of how they'd grown as a couple. Soon, she heard the sounds of a dial tone, biting her bottom lip. She hung up the phone to fall asleep in bed, thinking of how she could get back to her family without costing any more lives. Right across town at the same time, Chief Barrett was still at the station; it was well past midnight, and he'd still felt a little on edge, so he sat back with a glass of scotch in his hands while staring at the cell phone on his desk. Deciding to make a call he knew would possibly cost him his job or worse, he needed answers because things were unraveling. Gulping down the final remnants of his alcohol, he sighed, burping, lifting his phone, and punching in star sixty-nine.

"I told you I'd be in touch," the unknown voice spoke, feeling the aggravation in their tone. Sylvester cleared his throat, hoping things went better.

"We have a problem."

"I saw the news."

"This wasn't supposed to happen."

"Too late."

"This Agent Stone is causing more problems."

"Chief Barrett, are you drinking?"

"Any idea how this is going to work without me going to jail?"

Sylvester countered with a question of his own. Feeling worn down and agitated, he needed answers because he wasn't going down alone if it came to his livelihood. Sylvester's red-rim eyes would show the exhaustion in his face; the unbuttoned top of his uniform and disheveled hair showed the age lines of a man ready to retire. Only he wasn't a clean-cut, law-abiding police officer, not in his wife's eyes. After thirty years of marriage, he'd decided to step out with a few members of the local town, but Mrs. Barrett tried to work on keeping up the appearance they were a loving couple and family. He knew if what he was doing now came to light, she'd surely divorce him and leave town.

"Don't call me, and I'll call you, Chief Barrett."

Sylvester threw the glass across the room, shattering it, causing Bert to run in to see where the noise came from.

"Chief, you okay?" Bert burst through his office, scanning around the room, down at the shattered glass.

He stepped into his office, and the chief waved him off.

"I'm fine."

"Are you sure?"

"Yeah, just keep an eye on that Agent Stone for me."

"Uh, sir, she's FBI or something."

"Bert, do what I say."

"Yes, sir," Bert replied, leaving.

"Close the door."

"Yes, sir."

THREE

The whimpering of a soft voice with a blindfold covering their eyes, keeping them from seeing where they were, caused a tightness in the young girl's chest. She'd just left a party at a friend's house when she was walking home and caught the eye of a handsome young guy. Finally turning nineteen, she was hopeful to see what the dating life was like but getting inside his car showed it was a big mistake.

"Shush... your crying won't help you."

"Please... let me go."

"I can't do that."

"I won't tell anyone."

He knew that was true because his intentions of taking her became an extra bonus for him. Coming off a long day with clients, he needed to let off some steam, and the young beauty crossed his path. She looked young and untouched, so he expected to make a pretty penny from selling her to the highest bidder. Grabbing the empty tray off the floor, he stood back up and left her chained to the bed as she continued crying, wearing only a white gown he'd put on her after she was cleaned.

"Get some rest; you have a big day coming up."

"Please, let me go!" She tried to yank the chain off and felt it bruising her taut skin.

"In due time."

He shut the basement door, turned the lights out, and left her alone in a dingy bed, with no other form of escape. Crying herself to sleep, Gwen only thought about her family and how she'd wished she would have stayed home the other night.

After tossing the tray away and removing his gloves, he headed into his office and turned his computer on, checking for any signs that Gwen Akerson was missing. Normally, it would take a few days before anything would come across the radar, but since the other killings, he figured they'd ramped up surveillance. He smiled to himself that nothing was posted on TV or in the newspaper about his new prize possession. Tapping the numbers on his cell phone, he listened to the voice message coming through that stated his bank account had a deposit of fifty-thousand dollars. This was the smallest fee he had received for a client since it was a last-minute pickup. He wondered if his boss was getting too cocky with the increase in merchandise, but he wouldn't deal with that right now. His focus was on getting the girl transferred over so he could get back to his day job like nothing happened.

TWO DAYS LATER, in the middle of the afternoon, a woman stood behind Gwen, brushing her hair in a tight ponytail after bathing the dirt away. She'd placed a new white, strappy dress on the bed and sandals for her travels today. She'd been held in the same room, chained to the bed without a TV or fresh air from a window. All Gwen could do was cry herself to sleep and dream about her parents and little brother back home, afraid they'd never see her again.

"Where am I going?" Gwen whispered.

The older woman didn't speak English; she was just as much a victim as Gwen, but her freedom was contingent on being sent back to her country to be killed. Alejandra stood on the main road, trying to make money by selling flowers when an expensive Mercedes pulled up, and the gentleman offered her a job. She'd been with him for the past two years, and she regretted her decision every day. Never being able to go out or meet anyone like herself was torture; the only decent thing her boss provided was a bed and a bath-room of her own. With around-the-clock security and cameras sitting on the property, she would never be able to escape without someone catching and killing her.

"Can you..."

Gwen wiped her nose, giving up on trying to get her to understand what she was trying to say. The lock turned, and the door opened when security waved for Alejandra to bring the girl upstairs.

"What's happening? Please, someone, tell me."

"Shut up!" A tall security guard with limp and broad shoulders, standing at five-eleven, yelled.

"I want to go home." Gwen tried to jerk out of his hold as he guided her up the stairs and down the hallway.

"You're going to a new home," he snickered, tightening his grip on her arm.

Escorting Gwen out of the basement, and down the hallway, the guard checked to make sure her blindfold was still on. Her whimpers, and tears did nothing to change his mind of the job he's getting paid to do. His boss, stepped out of the kitchen. Drinking his cup of coffee, he watched as

Gwen was placed in the blue plumber van. He was dressed in his best black suit and admired his home with the living room encased in dark-grey colors, large open windows, and a massive fireplace with his name engraved. All of his accomplishments sat on top of the fireplace, and he couldn't wait for the excitement of securing more forbidden fruit.

"Boss, we're ready," another security guard spoke.

"Good, I'm ready for more fresh air."

"Are you bringing more girls?"

He turned, heading back into the kitchen to put the cup in the sink for Alejandra to clean.

"We might, but this time, you can test out what we find." He grinned, rubbing his hands together as the blond, six-feet-four guard smirked in excitement. He grabbed his coat and keys, exited the home, and jumped in the backseat of his chauffeur-driven Lincoln town car as the van pulled in behind them to follow. Checking the time on his watch, he wanted to set up a conference call with his other client, so he logged into his emails to see if any updates had come. The only way he'd lasted this long was by keeping everyone in suspense and never meeting at the same location. Falling under the radar had benefited, with no leaks or police knocking on his door. Stopping at the destination, he ended the call and stepped out of his car as the driver kept the engine running. Checking his tie while looking at the surrounding area of homes, he smiled and climbed the stairs to knock on the door. Hearing the locks, the door opened with a gun in his face and a smoke-filled room.

"Pull the van around back." the husky voice said.

He glanced over his shoulder, nodding to his security guard to drive to the back.

"Was she touched?" The short, brawny man lowered his gun and stepped to the side, allowing entrance.

The door closed, and he walked to the back, ignoring the question.

"The deal is almost done," the woman said, ending the phone call.

Pushing the door open of the one-story brick home, he stepped in as her men stood on both sides of the door with guns on their hips.

"Take a seat," she spoke.

"Cozy place."

She rolled her eyes, cupping her chin with both hands.

"I was surprised to get a call so quickly."

Unbuttoning his jacket, he crossed his leg with his hands clasped in front of him on his knee.

"I like to keep my clients happy."

She picked up a white envelope and tossed it across the desk.

"Fifty thousand."

"Thank you."

"You're not going to count, verify?"

"I know you wouldn't cross me."

"How do you know that?" Her eyes dipped low.

"You have too much to lose."

"That makes two of us."

"How is your boss?"

"Which one?"

"The one who keeps my bank account full?" He smiled smugly.

"Keeps providing what we need." She turned the monitor on the television, watching as Gwen was thrown into a bedroom as she cried out, wanting to be let go.

"When can I meet this boss?" he asked.

"Never." She walked around the desk, standing at its edge and running a hand across his shoulder.

"At some point, I'm going to want access."

"That will never happen, sorry." As she turned to walk back around to her desk, he gripped her wrist.

"Either you make it happen, or our business deal will dry up."

She looked down at his hand and jerked away with a scowl on her face.

"You don't want to threaten me; it would be bad for your business and your health."

"Only a matter of time before cops find out about your second job."

"Before or after you tell them?" she asked.

Turning the monitor off, she placed the remote down.

"Keep up this facade, but the second you get in trouble, I bet your boys will bail out on you."

She laughed at his comment.

"Doubt that."

"Why's that?"

"Being family comes with its perks."

He smirked at his reply.

"When can you get more girls?" she questioned.

"I don't know. With the killings, I can't be sure your boss won't fuck up again."

"A little carried away; it won't happen again."

"How many more?"

"At least five if possible. We have some overseas partners interested."

"So, is Gwen a personal one for him?"

"That's not your concern."

Rising out of the chair, he peered at her, watching as her pupils elevated, showing she was hiding something.

"If anything traces back to me..."

"Has anything come back on you?" She threw her hands up in the air.

"Remember to keep it that way."

"We might have something I need you to keep an eye on."

"What?"

"The chief called about visitors in town to handle investigating the deaths."

"Chief is your problem."

"Yet you're going to help because Agent Stone is asking questions."

"Still want to keep your big boss out of this, but you're requesting my help."

He leaned forward.

"From what I read, she's good at her job."

"What do you want me to do?"

"Kill her."

"That's going to cost you."

"Tell me something I didn't know."

"I have a busy day, already running behind. I'll be in touch." He pushed the envelope inside his trench coat pocket, heading toward the door.

"Remember, I need more girls asap," she called out.

Glancing over his shoulder, he acknowledged, "Yes, ma'am."

She smiled, sitting back down in her chair and turning the monitor back on.

"Your tears will dry soon," she muttered.

She knew disobeying her boss and letting Agent Stone get too close would not only destroy their career, but her life would be even more in danger. Putting up a front a few minutes ago, her throat felt constricted at the thought of being on their bad side.

FOUR

Stepping into Gwen Akerson's family home, Teagan and Spider felt conflicted at having to deal with a family's anguish, but they needed answers on how Gwen went about the day when they spoke to her last. Watching all the police cars outside of the house, Chief Barrett let them know how the family called as soon as they realized she never came home.

"Take the lead," Teagan told Spider.

"Are you sure?"

Teagan nodded, watching as Mrs. Akerson wiped her tears away, and her husband held her in his arms. Watching as Spider went toward the couple, she scanned the room and stayed back, keeping her eyes on the entire room. A few of the police officers whispered amongst themselves about Teagan and her team coming into town and trying to take over.

"Mr. and Mrs. Akerson, I'm very sorry to bother you."

"Have you found our daughter?" Mr. Akerson questioned.

She scanned the magazines sitting on the coffee table,

taking in the homey feel that was probably full of laughter and love before Gwen was taken.

"No, ma'am. I'm Agent Hitchson and my partner Agent Stone." Spider held his badge out, pointing at Teagan.

"The chief said that you're from the FBI?" She held her hands up in prayer.

"Something like that," Spider responded.

"How can we help bring our baby home?" Mr. Akerson asked.

With a knock at their door, Officer Copeland walked inside, holding his helmet.

"Michelle, Doug, I'm so sorry about Gwen." Peter went further into the living room, bent down, and hugged Michelle, as long-time friends of the family. He brought comfort none of the other officers could do.

"Thanks for coming, Peter." Doug waved for him to have a seat on the chair opposite Spider.

"It's pretty clear we're dealing with professionals," Peter stated.

"Officer Copeland, I'd prefer we didn't give out any details on the suspects," Spider mentioned.

"I'm just keeping my friends updated," Peter replied.

"I understand, but we don't want to give false information," Spider said.

"Maybe we could give them money," Michelle blurted out.

"Situations like this don't normally revolve around money," Spider said.

"Mrs. Akerson, has Gwen had any fights or arguments with anyone lately?" Teagan asked.

Peter chewed on his bottom lip, scowling at Teagan. He pushed out a breath, picking up the Bible lying on the end table.

"Not that I believe. Gwen's a good girl."

"What about school? Any boyfriends that might be able to help?" Spider picked up on Teagan's questioning.

"My daughter didn't have a boyfriend," Doug said.

"Can you provide a list of friends?" Spider asked.

"We gave that to the police already." Michelle sighed.

"I understand. It's just—"

"She said she already gave it to our team," Peter interrupted.

"Mr. Copeland, do you mind if we speak outside for a moment?" Teagan pointed at the front door. Peter looked annoyed at being summoned to step outside as Doug and Michelle looked on. Teagan held the door open as she waited. Closing the door, she stepped into his face.

"Mr. Copeland, I'm not going to repeat myself."

"Watch how you speak to me, lady." He looked around, making sure no one was watching the exchange.

"Agent Stone to you, and respect goes both ways."

"Fine, I need to get back in there."

Peter turned to leave, but Teagan held a hand up to block him.

"The only way you can help your friends is by cooperating with my team."

"Don't try to tell me how to do my job."

"Would you rather we leave, and more girls end up dead?"

"I know this family. Gwen wouldn't just take off," Peter explained.

"Which could be true, but until we have all of the evidence, nothing's ruled out."

Gathering that she could be correct, Peter decided to stop fighting her to take control of the case and would step back until he saw they'd overstepped the line.

"The chief wants me to follow this case to make sure nothing is missed."

"I can assure you, nothing will be missed. My team's record will show that we always close a case." Teagan headed back inside as Peter watched on in a tempered attitude.

While Spider continued talking with the couple, Teagan went to Gwen's bedroom, opening the door. She noticed everything was neat and clean. Her bedroom held a bed, desk, with Justin Bieber posters hanging around the room. Clothes were neatly piled on her bed that looked fresh and clean. Stepping to the desk, she saw pictures of Gwen with a few friends in cheerleader outfits, posing in front of a football field. Scanning her desk, she noticed books and papers. Lifting her pen, she sifted through the documents to find anything outstanding. Mainly notes from class and homework.

"Where are you, Gwen?" she muttered to herself.

Meeting Spider back in the truck a few minutes later, he shut the door, passing her the list of friends that her parents compiled.

"What did you say to that cop?"

"Nothing I wouldn't say to anyone on our team."

Looking over at her, he smirked.

"He completely changed his attitude when he came back and was more helpful."

Teagan shrugged her shoulders, checking all three names.

"These are the same names that police already provided."

"Yeah, I think we can finish talking with them today and maybe look for a connection."

Moving through town, Teagan watched as everyone

went on about their business, not feeling any disturbance from a local killer being in town.

BACK AT THE STATION, a few hours later, Teagan, Spider, and Daughtrey were reading through the material they'd compiled since taking over the case. Connecting the number of missing girls over the past few weeks, she calculated a total of five, between the ages of twelve and twenty-two. Tracking the drop-offs at the barn from each person's home, there wasn't a rhyme or reason for why the girls were chosen, beyond being able to be controlled.

"You think we'll find a pattern before he strikes again?" Daughtrey asked.

"What makes you think it's a man?" Spider replies.

Teagan looked at the question.

"What did you say?"

"I said—"

She raised her hand.

"Not you. Spider."

"What? Makes you think it's a man," Spider repeated.

"That's it." Teagan jumped up and went to the white-board, picking up the black sharpie and making a list.

"What are you doing?" Daughtrey questioned as he leaned back, scratching the side of his face.

Teagan drew a line from each location where the girls were abducted to the land field.

"All were picked up and held for a few days before being dumped at the field."

Spider looked at the medical papers.

"At least a week or two," Spider said.

"So, whoever is doing this somehow gets bored or annoyed."

"We could probably put a team on the field to investigate if they come back," Daughtrey mentioned.

"What time did the coroner say they died?"

Flipping through the binder on the table, Spider repeated the time for the first three girls.

"Let's have local police sit at the location." Teagan was about to mark on the whiteboard again when a knock came at the door. The mayor walked in with Bert behind him.

"Agent Stone, I wanted to check on the progress of the case," Mayor Henton said.

"The case is coming along. We've met with the Akersons."

"Has Copeland been helpful?"

Bert stared at Teagan with his lip curved upwards, anticipating the answer. Spider and Daughtrey watched the exchange between the two.

"Copeland and I have an understanding now."

Henton reached inside his jacket and pulled out an envelope, handing it to Teagan.

"What's this?" She opened the envelope, pulling out two tickets.

"Those are tickets to the fundraiser the governor is throwing in a few weeks."

"Does he know who we are?"

"No, I had extra tickets, and I wanted to bring you as guests," Henton replied.

"Thank you," Teagan said.

Teagan passed the tickets over to Spider.

"Tell me about the governor," she said.

"He's one of those established politicians," Henton remarked.

"Officer Bert, do you mind bringing us the school records of Gwen Akerson?" Teagan asked, wanting to delve deeper into the governor's life without anyone finding out.

"That's not my job," Bert scoffed.

"Officer, either you're going to perform your duties, or you're not," Henton argued.

"Yes, sir," Bert replied.

Bert walked out of the room.

"He's a peach," Daughtrey blurted out.

"So, Governor Snyder."

"Every year, these fundraisers happen, and he invites the local leaders that have long family ties in politics," Mayor Henton recalled.

"Is he married?" Teagan glanced at the mayor.

Spider typed on his computer.

"For at least twenty years, three kids," Spider said.

"You're not thinking Snyder has anything to do with this?" Henton said.

"I keep all options open. Whoever is behind these killings has an extensive reach."

"I understand, but the governor wouldn't be behind something this dark."

"Has your assistant sent over all the documents I requested?"

She needed the list of local businesses that used to be in the surrounding areas near the farm.

"I asked her to give you whatever you needed."

"We haven't heard from her," Spider replied.

"Okay, I'll get on that. But please remember to try not to ruffle any feathers."

"Based on my background, sir, I can't promise to not push people's buttons."

Thinking over the invite as Henton left the room,

Teagan wanted to make a lasting impression on the governor, better than she did the chief. It was getting later in the day, and the chief wanted to get an update from her before she went back to the hotel. Gathering up her notes, she left Spider and Daughtrey to finish gathering more evidence.

Strolling down the hallway of the station, Teagan passed Bert and Copeland talking together in the corner. They peered at her as she knocked on the chief's door. Hearing she could come in, Teagan took a long breath, released it, and smiled as she pushed the door open.

"Chief."

"Have a seat, Agent Stone."

"Thank you."

"How are things with the hotel you're staying at?"

Taken aback by his question, she paused before answering.

"Okay."

"I hear your whole team is coming along with the investigation."

"We are."

"Do you have any updates I can give the families?"

He tapped the pen across the desk, waiting for an answer.

"After speaking with the Akersons, I want to wait before doing anything that will tip off anyone."

"So you think you've found the person?" he probed further.

"No, the mayor was getting more documents sent to my team."

"As you can tell, I'm in a bind."

Seeing the stress lines over his forehead, Teagan was tempted to ask if he was being paid by somebody to answer even if it wasn't correct.

"Chief, is everything okay?"

The chief opened his desk drawer, pulled out a bottle of Pepto Bismol, poured a small amount in a cup, and drank it down.

"Stomach virus."

Seeing the sweat pooled together and eyes jumping from around the room, Teagan was skeptical it was only a virus. Since getting the call, the team had been hit with roadblocks non-stop.

"Maybe you should take some time off."

Coughing, he nodded in agreement.

"Listen, I have to do a press conference soon, and I need something."

"Call it off."

"I can't do that."

"You would be playing into their hands."

"Agent, we have dead girls in my town. I need someone to blame!" he shouted.

"That hasn't left my mind, sir."

Teagan jumped up, pointing at herself.

Pushing back from the desk, Chief Snyder stood, crossing his arms over his chest.

"Either I have something for the news by the end of the week, or I'll call to get you replaced."

"Try it now." Teagan grabbed the receiver off the phone and dialed the number at the Agency.

"Director's office," a woman said over the phone.

"Can you get the person who's in charge on the phone, please?"

"Agent Stone, is that you?" she asked.

"Yes, it's me."

"Is everything all right?"

"Chief would like to know if I could be replaced." Teagan stared into his eyes as she spoke.

"Ummm... I doubt it since you're the director of The Agency and in charge of everyone."

"Thank you, Caroline." Teagan pushed to end the call.

"Chief, your wife's out front, complaining," Bert barked, pushing his door open without waiting to be asked.

Chief muttered, "Shit, I told her not to come back up here."

"Do you mind if I use your phone? I need to check in with my family." Teagan asked. She could see he was about to decline her but decided against it.

"Yeah, just don't hog up the line," the chief replied, treading out of the room. Bert stood at the door as Teagan lifted the phone.

"It's private."

He smirked, a cocky and devilish sort of expression as he closed the door.

Dialing Gregory's number, Teagan watched through the blinds as the chief argued back and forth with his wife at the front counter. While waiting for the call to go through, Teagan rose toward the computer screen, seeing it was already open with his email and a few files, including the case.

"Gregory," he said.

"Gregory, this is Teagan."

"I was tracing this call, wondering if one of you guys had gotten into trouble."

He chuckled. Teagan chortled.

"No, but the chief had to step out for a moment, and I needed to call my family."

"What do you need?" he asked.

"Trace his computer and phone log."

"How far back?"

"At least six months."

Teagan ran her hand across the mouse, keeping an eye on the chief and Bert. Clicking on the emails that talked about the case, she mainly saw news requests and local councilmen wanting to know how things were going. Another email had popped up two minutes before she came into his office to talk.

"I'll need a little bit of time."

"Rush job," she said, clicking and opening the email.

Friend: Event tickets are sold out.

Chief: You do this every time.

Friend: Then you should do what they tell you next time.

"Gotcha, boss."

"What is—" The chief rushed back into his office with his wife beside him as Teagan quickly logged out of his email.

"I'll be home soon, honey." Teagan hung the phone up, rising out of the chief's seat.

"Who are you?" his wife asked.

Teagan extended her hand for a shake.

"Agent Stone, ma'am."

"Are you sleeping with my husband too?" she blurted out, swaying left to right.

"Ignore my wife; she likes to drink a little more at lunch than her friends," Chief groaned, nudging his wife to sit.

"I'll be in touch, Chief." Teagan reached for the knob, then a cold, still voice came from behind.

"At least try to be more discreet, Agent Stone."

Rushing down the hallway, Teagan slowly closed the door, keeping an eye on everyone in the precinct.

"You look like you've seen a ghost," Daughtrey commented nervously.

"I met the chief's wife, and something felt off about her."

"What do you mean?" Spider questioned.

Ignoring the question, Teagan ran a hand down her face.

"I spoke with Gregory, and he's going to trace the last few calls from the chief's desk."

Daughtrey and Spider both peered at the revelation.

"You think the chief is behind this?" Daughtrey whispered.

"Not sure, but I can't rule out anyone. Let's wrap up for the night and get back to the hotel."

"Camden, Nebraska has just as many secrets as Wall Street," Daughtrey mumbled.

Grabbing the brush and cleaning off the whiteboard, Teagan continued to stare at the location they found the bodies for a few extra seconds before cleaning it off.

FIVE

One week later back in DC.

Senator Steinman sat back in her office, fielding requests for the upcoming budget bill the president had planned out. She wanted to cut it by one trillion and proposed other options to try to have a bipartisan bill for the American people. She felt President Sanders only wanted to appease his base and not make the hard choices. Martha Steinman is a senator from Tennessee in office for the past ten years, working to establish her career as a hardliner on crime and pro-business. As a woman in her late fifties, married with four children, she knew what it took to be the only woman in the room. That's why going through the budget and seeing the funding for certain Defense spending caused a red flag. A knock at her door paused her reading as she called for the person to come in and have a seat.

"Senator Steinman."

He extended a hand.

"Secretary Kelton."

Waving at the chair in front of her desk, she nodded for him to sit.

"To what do I owe this visit, sir."

Smiling, Todd loosened his jacket, picking up a piece of peppermint off her desk.

"Well, I know you're working on the budget for the president."

"That's right."

"As secretary of transportation, I wanted to see if we could help each other out."

"How can I help you?"

"President Sanders won't be in office for much longer."

"Are you planning on running?"

"Something I'm considering."

"You're in his cabinet. Won't he see this as a betrayal?"

"We've never agreed on much, but this is a political move."

Todd Kelton was the snake oil type of politician; his family had a long line of political stature that he ran on. At forty years old, he was young, married with two kids, and considered one of *People Magazine*'s politicians to watch. Before taking on the transportation role, he worked on Wall Street, making millions, and decided to move into politics after seeing all of the regulations Sanders was trying to push through legislation. Running on bipartisanship to get Sanders on his side was the first step to gain his trust.

"Why should I believe you? I mean, the media says you're the one behind all of Sanders' decisions."

He chuckled at her statement.

"Sanders has no political clout left; he's run this country into the ground."

"That we can agree on. You know this budget he's proposing is outrageous."

"I heard he has funds for a certain department that's now under the Pentagon."

Martha's eyes widened in surprise.

"The Firm."

"An agency that's not to be touched. But I think we could dismantle it if done right."

"How?"

"Do I have your support?"

Martha nodded.

"Do what you do best; get them in front of the committee."

"You mean for a hearing?"

"Yes, while they're distracted. Sanders won't have time to handle everything."

"His chief of staff would point to someone in charge."

"Not if you make it where they have a last-minute distraction and set the meeting last minute."

"I don't know, Kelton."

"What are you afraid of, Martha?"

"I follow the constitution. No one is above the law."

He smirked.

"Discretion is something you'll learn very early on with me, Senator."

"Nobody in the history of the Senate committee has pulled this off."

"Until today."

"What do I have as insurance that you won't cross me like you're doing to Sanders?"

Todd gave her a knowing smile and reached his palm out. Martha looked from his hand up to his face and back. Shaking hands, Martha wondered if she was making the right decision in what the secretary was pledging as a partnership.

"What do you want, Senator?"

"I want Speaker."

"Aiming high, I see."

"As you can see, I'm putting my name out there, and more than likely will take the fall on this if we fail."

"There's something else I need."

Martha scoffed, throwing her pen down.

"What else?"

"There's a case in Nebraska—"

"Excuse me, Senator, you have a call on line four," her secretary said.

"Thank you, Krystal. Mr. Kelton emailed me about the Nebraska case."

Todd held a hard glare across his face watching Martha take a call while he was trying to set his plans in motion.

"Okay. Thank you, Senator."

She waved goodbye to him as he left her office. Heading out of the building, Todd cracked his knuckles and adjusted his tie. Security held the door open, and Todd slid in, sitting across from another associate.

"What did she say?"

"She's on board."

"You think we can trust her?"

The limo drove out of the parking lot into traffic. He broke his gaze from looking at the people walking around.

"I can't trust you, let alone anyone else."

"Are you upset?"

"I need another one."

"What happened to the last one I gave you?"

"She's dead!" he snapped.

Sweat beads pooled at his forehead.

"Todd, you promised no more killing."

Ten minutes later, the car stopped at the Barton Restaurant near 11 St. and West. Stepping out of the car, Todd looked around the area. Before he sauntered into the restaurant, he requested to be shut down.

"Mr. Secretary, your table is ready." Melinda said.

"Thank you, Melinda."

The grey-blue-eyed, blonde-haired hostess escorted him toward the private room, with his guest waiting. A few seconds later, his other passenger arrived.

"Make this quick. I shouldn't be seen with you."

"I take it our mutual colleague explained about this meeting."

"Mr. Keenan, you have five minutes of my time."

"Can I get you a drink, sir?" the hostess asked.

"No," Todd answered.

"I'll take another whiskey neat," Neal stated.

"Coming right up."

The hostess left them to continue their conversation. Todd Kelton didn't like to be summoned. His brow raised in suspicion.

"Extremely impressed you've been able to last this long."

"Is that a threat?" Todd's breathing heightened in frustration.

"Mr. Kelton, I would never put you at risk or myself that way."

"Keep it that way."

"Aren't you married with children?" Neal asked.

All eyes stared at Todd.

"None of your concern."

"Touché. But I propose a little help from you."

"What type of help?"

"The type that could be very rewarding for you and for me."

"In what way?" The hostess stepped back in the room

as the waitress brought out Neal's plate filled with vegetables and steak.

"Neal works for the governor," she said.

"Does he know about me?" Todd questioned, pointing at himself.

Not wanting to waste any more time, Neal had to get an agreement signed before anyone found out what he'd planned next.

"No, I have just as much to lose as you, Secretary."

Drinking his whiskey, Neal sighed, letting the taste linger and mesh with the flavors of the steak.

"I have cargo coming in on the harbor, and I'd like to have you clear it without hassle."

"You're kidding, right?"

"Do I look like I'm kidding?"

"What type of cargo?"

"Cargo you like, Secretary Kelton."

A glint in his eyes sparkled when Neal confessed more girls were coming soon.

"How many?" Todd whispered.

"Thirty," Neal replied.

"When are they coming?" Todd licked his lips.

"Sir, remember you promised no more threats," she told him.

Loosening his tie, glancing over his shoulder, Todd waved for the waitress to come back over.

"Sir, can I get you something?" Melinda asked.

"I'll have a whiskey and steak, please," he responded, grinning at the smirk on Neal's face.

Neal raised his glass in a toast. This would be the most girls he'd brought to the country under these travels.

"You'll need to make sure nothing traces back to me."

"We're in agreement, Senator. I work for the governor, so this is between you and me."

"How much are we talking about for my cut?" she queried, hoping she could finally end working for Henton and leave the country with the money she'd saved.

"For setting up this meeting, I can do maybe twenty thousand," Todd said.

She studied him for a moment, with the audacity to only offer twenty thousand when he more than likely made close to half a million from bringing those girls.

"Let me rephrase; I want a hundred grand in my account."

Todd chuckled at her request, leaning closer and whispering, "I'm not giving you a hundred thousand dollars."

"Secretary Kelton, we both know what you like."

Twirling the butter knife on the table, Todd knew she was taking advantage of the situation and wouldn't hesitate to rat him out. He needed to get rid of her before the deal was complete and work straight through Neal going forward.

"Let me think of my options."

"Either you come up with the money, or you find someone who does."

"I can't just transfer that much money without my wife noticing."

Pulling out his ringing phone, Neal answers the call from the governor.

"Governor, is everything all right?" Neal asked.

Todd waited as Neal continued his conversation.

"Will do, sir." Neal hung up the phone.

"What does he want?" she questioned.

"About his fundraiser tomorrow."

"Are you flying back for that?" She watched as Neal gathered his wallet and left money on the table.

"Yeah, in fact, I need to leave in the next five minutes," Neal responded.

He extended his hand toward Secretary Kelton.

"Mr. Secretary, I'll be in contact about Washington Ports."

Kelton shook his hand and watched as he left the room.

"You might think I'm trying to take advantage of the situation, but I want out."

"You're out when I say you're out." Todd jumped up out of his chair, stomped out of the restaurant, and headed back to the limo as she scrambled to follow. She tried to slide in next to him, but he blocked her from entering.

"Take a cab." He slammed the door, motioning for security to drive off.

ARRIVING HOME THIRTY MINUTES LATER, he said goodbye for the night as he entered the mansion of his home, hearing his kids laughing and playing. Undoing his tie, he removed his jacket and went to the bar in the corner of his living room, almost tripping over the toy police car.

"Fuck!" He kicked the car against the wall.

Grabbing the bourbon off the counter, he poured the glass up to the rim and drank it down in one gulp.

Rubbing the back of his neck, Todd continued staring at his children's toys on the ground. Hearing the rumbling of his stomach, he started to go toward the kitchen when his wife and son came into the room.

"I didn't know you were home," Liz said, running into

his arms, standing on her tippy toes, and wrapping her arms around his neck.

"Surprise." He pecked her lips and ruffled his son's hair.

TJ was the spitting image of him with his blonde hair and blue eyes.

"Daddy, can I go to the carnival?" TJ asked.

Todd bent down and cupped his son's chin.

"Were you good for Mommy while I was gone?"

TJ grinned, nodding his head. Todd shifted his head as his other children came into the room talking with each other. His heart beat faster seeing the chaos moving around him.

"Did you miss me?"

"Every minute," Todd replied, standing.

SIX

The gun cocked back as her mind filled with every scenario that could go wrong if she didn't find out who was behind the death of two more girls—dressed in a green silk dress with thin straps and a low-cut, V-neck slit, and high heels. She checked her makeup one more time in the mirror and wondered how Christian would feel about her going undercover as someone who was going to buy girls. She smoothed her black fur coat over her dress, pulling her red lace front wig forward, seeing the hazel contact lenses and red full lips glowing under the car light. Her maturity at thirty-six was showcased as her mind games had grown beyond the first time she went undercover.

"Remember we can hear everything," Gregory mentioned.

"I shouldn't be more than an hour or two unless the conversation moves to business."

Pulling up to the exclusive party at the governor's home, the valet opened Teagan's door as Spider stepped out alongside her in his black tuxedo. Placing her hand on his arm, she smiled at the valet and watched as Sean went to park with Gregory still in the car. Daughtrey and Broderick followed in the second van and parked a block away, watching as cars came and went. Hearing the classical music from inside, Spider tightened his hold on Teagan's arm, helping her up the steps of the home. Butlers stood with both doors open in the twenty-thousand-square-foot, two-story home. Walking in, the pictures of previous governors hung on the wall, with expensive artwork alongside. Waitstaff stood with a tray of champagne glasses for them to take, and both declined, wanting to keep a clear head as they went in to meet the wealthy elite of Nebraska. Gold marble floors were inscribed with the governor's name, and a statue of his face sat near his family photo. You could tell he thought highly of himself and came from money like Mayor Henton, but he didn't use his name as a stepping-stone to further his career.

"Ready for this?" Spider released the hold on Teagan's arm, scanning the room of people talking in huddles of groups.

"Try not to get into any trouble." Teagan winked, removing her fur coat and passing it to the staff. She pressed her clenched purse to her stomach. Lifting the corners of her lips, she smiled, moving into the crowd as she swished around the room, waiting for someone to take the bait as her curves swayed in her gown. After three kids, she only got more and more beautiful as she aged with constantly working out and running behind her children. Surprisingly, the kids wanted more siblings after all these years, and she explained that wasn't happening. Even with having a dog, the house was always busy with noise.

"Excuse me, do I know you?" Teagan shifted, looking behind her at the voice calling out to her. Never knowing who she'd met throughout her time undercover, she couldn't remember the man with olive skin, short, dark hair, and six-four height.

"I don't; I'm Patricia Langston." Teagan reached her hand over for him to shake.

"You're extremely beautiful, Patricia. I'm Adam Gardner." The firm handshake and mischievous smile on his face set off high alerts that could lead her to some answers.

"Thank you."

"Are you here with anyone?" Adam brought the champagne glass to his lips.

"I have a friend here with me."

"A friend who would say something about me speaking with you."

"Depends on what the conversation is about."

Adam stepped in closer to Teagan, bent down, and whispered in her ear.

"My gut is telling me you'd like my conversation."

Teagan cocked her head to the left, grinning at Adam and licking her lips.

"What do you do for a living, Adam?" A waitstaff came over with a tray of shrimp wraps in kale.

"No, thank you," Teagan said.

"I'm an investor. What about you?" Adam placed the champagne down and took a second one from the tray.

"Same."

"Are you on Travis' payroll?" Adam questioned, glancing at Governor Snyder standing with his wife on his arm.

"No, I was invited because we have a few things in common."

"Really, like what?"

"If I tell you, I'd have to kill you." Teagan winked,

starting to head over to the governor and his wife when Adam grasped her hand.

"Maybe I'm intrigued."

"I doubt what I'm into is something you'd be interested in."

"What gives you that idea?"

Staring at Travis, Teagan noticed when he tried to place his hand on his wife's lower back, and she smacked it away. Not wanting to be embarrassed, Travis cleared his throat, calling for another drink. A waitstaff made an announcement that dinner would be ready in five minutes.

"Mr. Gardner, my extra investments are sometimes off the books." Teagan remained calm, steadfast in her speaking. Erring on the side of caution, she wanted to ease him into explaining what he was into.

"Most of the people here work off the books."

"I see."

"What if we go somewhere private and talk?"

She glanced around the room, making eye contact with Spider, letting him know she was moving, and keeping an eye on everyone.

"Following your lead, Mr. Gardner."

"Call me Adam." He motioned for her to walk ahead of him as he put his champagne down and headed toward the balcony. The palace was booming with music, photographers taking pictures, and staff roaming around trying to keep things in order. Teagan estimated there were about a hundred or more guests at his home. Nodding to the women glaring at her as she sashayed outside, she chuckled at the annoyance but didn't care to address it at this moment. Tapping her thigh to make sure the gun was still within reach, Teagan turned around as Adam closed the double balcony doors behind them.

"Are you married, Patricia?"

Adam approached her with her back toward the railing.

"No, are you?"

"A man like me can't settle down. A woman wouldn't understand my needs."

"What are those needs, Mr. Gardner?"

Adam trailed his palm across her wrist, up her arm to lift her chin, making direct eye contact.

"Have dinner with me and find out."

Teagan reached up and took his hand in hers, moving it away gently.

"Only thing I'm interested in is business, Adam. I don't mix it with pleasure."

"I could change your mind; I'm known to have women groveling at my feet."

"Sounds spicy, but I love money more."

Adam chuckled. "Then we could get along fine."

"What business dealings do you have with Snyder?" Tegan ran her palm up to his chest.

"Snyder and I go way back from our college days. He's money-hungry like me."

"From looking at his home, I can see that."

"Listen, let's cut to the chase and get down to what we can do for each other, Patricia."

"I'm all ears."

"I have a few clubs I invest in and rental property."

Teagan fell back in laughter.

"You think a little club money is what I want?" Teagan started to push Adam to the side and walk off.

"Wait... I might have more ways to get money."

She closed the space between them and pursed her lips.

"Good, I hope it's something worth my time."

"Some of my friends have their hands in things outside of the legal realm."

"Dinner is being served," a waitress interrupted their conversation.

Putting space between them, Teagan stepped back, smiling at the waitress, and started to head back into the home toward the dinner party. Adam was impressed with the way her ass sat in the dress and wanted to get to the dark beauty more, but he knew divulging all his secrets early would probably put him in a bad spot with the governor and his clients. Seeing all of the guests sitting and talking with the governor at the head of the table, Teagan looked for Spider and noticed him sitting at the edge of the table. Right as she walked over, Adam grasped her hand. Teagan was startled for a moment and looked back at Adam.

"We should continue our conversation unless you're occupied with someone else."

Shaking her head no, she took him up on his offer and followed him to the empty seats near Governor Snyder. Sitting down, she placed the napkin on her leg and lifted the glass of water.

"Adam, I see you've found a friend," Snyder said, leaning over the table.

His wife Juliette rolled her eyes and continued drinking as the food was being brought out.

"This is Patricia Langston, Governor." Adam introduced me.

"Lovely to meet you, Patricia. I'm Travis Snyder." He held her palm in his hand, kissing the back of her knuckle.

"I'm his wife Juliette, but you wouldn't know that with how much of an asshole—"

"Juliette, this is not the time," Travis grunted; the grimace on her face showed she hated Travis Snyder.

"Nice to meet you, Governor. Adam has been telling me a lot about you and your beautiful wife."

Teagan studied them both, analyzing the posture and body language between the couple. If she had to bet, the marriage was just for convenience, and both of them were probably cheating on each other and only showing love in front of the cameras. Travis stood and clanked the butterknife against his glass to get everyone's attention.

"Ladies and gentlemen, thank you so much for joining us tonight.""

Spider continued taking in everybody and allowing his hidden camera on his tie to scan faces to send back to Gregory to investigate.

"As governor, your support has been wonderful and truly appreciated."

"Another campaign run!" someone shouted out.

Travis chuckled, shaking his head at the outburst from his campaign manager Neal Keenan. She had to give it to him—Travis came off very charming and outgoing.

"Well, that's something I will talk about at another time. Tonight is about celebrating our wins." Travis and the other guests raised a glass as he gave a toast.

"To us," Travis said, staring at Teagan, lifting his drink and smirking. She didn't think he could recognize her with the heavy makeup and contacts in her eyes, so she hoped by the end of the night, more secrets would be spilled.

AN HOUR LATER, everybody was at the point of hungover from dinner and relaxed, so Teagan took that as an opportunity to look around. Governor Snyder was whispering in his wife's ear, Neal texted on his phone as the other guests talked back and forth.

"I need to use the restroom," she said, dropping her napkin on the table and pushing the chair back to step away.

"I can show you." Adam stood from his seat. Teagan planted her hand on his shoulder, stopping him from following. Teagan smoothly rubbed her palm across his shoulder, shaking her head no, and glanced up at Travis as he explained to turn left and down the hallway to the bathroom on the right. Carrying her purse, she swished out of the dining room, passing the portrait of Snyder shaking hands with Mayor Henton. Peering back, she checked to make sure no one else was coming as she continued toward the restroom, going past a closet left ajar. Seeing the bathroom next to another door, she placed her ear against the door to hear if anyone was inside. Gripping the door handle, she slowly turned the knob, finding it open. Glancing over her shoulder one more time, she slipped through the door, shutting it lightly. Feeling the wall, she came across a painting made of Governor Snyder. The room was dark brown with a leather loveseat, chess table, mahogany wooden desk, and world globe sitting in the corner near a trophy stand. Teagan went to the drawers, opening one by one, seeing old receipts and memos of meetings. Clicking the keyboard, the monitor popped onto the Internet Explorer, and moving the mouse over to the file folder, it was clear of any information stored.

"I'm tired of you flirting in front of me, Travis," a voice snapped.

Surprised at the voices arguing, she mumbled under her breath and tiptoed to the door, listening.

"Calm down, baby. You know I only want you," Snyder replied.

"Then tell your wife." she fussed.

Teagan's eyes peered down at the doorknob as it rotated, and the door opened slightly. She moved against the back corner of the door, out of sight.

"Come in—" Governor Snyder said.

"Travis, what are you doing?" Juliette asked, interrupting him at the door with his mistress. Teagan held her breath, hoping he didn't step further into the room and blow her cover.

"Missy needed to use the phone," Travis stated.

"She can use the one in the kitchen with the help. I mean, she does help you in some way," Juliette remarked.

"Juliette," Travis barked.

"It's okay, Travis," Missy said.

Travis' hand held the door open for another second.

"I'll show you to the kitchen, Missy," Travis told her.

"We both can, darling," Juliette responded.

Shutting the door closed, Teagan released the long-held breath and waited until the footsteps went away. Peeking through the door, she went out and slid over to the bathroom. Five minutes later, she came out of the bathroom and strolled back into the dining room. Seeing dessert placed on the table, Teagan motioned, moving her hand up her arm, letting Spider know she was ready to end the night. As soon as he stood, Teagan cleared her throat, getting everyone's attention.

"Mr. Governor, I had a lovely time, but it's past my bedtime, I'm afraid."

"You're leaving so soon." Governor Snyder held onto her palm, making circles against her knuckles gently.

"I must get to work early." Teagan slid her hand out.

"What are you doing?"

"Investments and some of the book business," she bent down and whispered in his ear.

"You should speak with my campaign manager; I could use more investments."

"Give me a call." Teagan opened her clutch, taking out a business card as Spider slid her coat around her shoulders.

"Can I walk you out?" Adam asked.

Spider and Teagan looked at each other briefly.

"I'd like that."

Adam approached, holding out his hand, and Teagan took it, walking alongside him out of the door, with Spider stalking behind. The butler held the door open as their car arrived to take them home. Teagan licked her lips as Adam stared into her eyes.

"I'd love to take you out for dinner," Adam said.

"I don't date."

Spider got in the right passenger side, shutting the door, grabbing the seatbelt.

"We can discuss the business information."

"That depends on what information you have for me." Teagan lifted her right leg about to hop in when Adam placed his hand on her lower back, stopping her.

"I know who can help you."

"Okay, how can they help me?" she questioned.

"Meet me here tomorrow at four." Adam pulled out his business card and pen, writing down an address.

Teagan spiked her left brow up in curiosity.

"If this is only about you having sex with me, Adam..."

"I promise, all business."

"We'll see." She got in the car, shutting the door, calling out for them to leave.

Spider turned his head as she reached under her dress

for her gun that was holstered to her thigh. Also taking out her cell phone, Teagan contacted Broderick and Daughtrey.

"What do you think?" she asked Spider as she tossed her wig off, slid out of her heels, and changed into tights, a large t-shirt, and sneakers.

"We didn't get anything major," Gregory called out.

"Anything on your end, Broderick?"

"All license plates checked out clean," Broderick replied.

"Travis is having an affair, but nothing jumped out when I went to his office."

It started sprinkling as the car pulled up to the hotel. Holding the phone in her hand, she looked out of the window and saw Broderick pull in behind them. Ending the call, Teagan jumped out of the car and ran inside, throwing the gown and wig in the trashcan next to the elevator. Stepping on the elevator with the rest of the team, she stared at the makeup on her face through the elevator door.

Getting off on their floor, everyone marched toward their room door in thought. Removing the key from her pocket, Teagan unlocked the door and stepped in, throwing her things on the couch. Kicking off her shoes, she plopped on the bed, blowing out a breath and turning to her side. Staring at her purse for over five minutes, she got off the bed and checked for the business card Adam offered, noticing the other business card of Snyder's campaign manager. Flicking her finger against each card, Teagan sat back down on the bed and peered at the time on the clock.

"Four tomorrow," she whispered.

SEVEN

Turning off the shower, Neal grabbed the towel off the back of the door. Scanning the business suits in his bedroom closet, he thought about his meeting with Governor Snyder in an hour. After getting dressed and walking downstairs to his kitchen to fix his tie, Alejandra placed a cup of coffee in front of his bowl of oatmeal.

"Alejandra, I'm going to be late for dinner tonight."

"Yes, sir."

"Is our guest awake?"

"Yes, sir."

"Good."

Finishing his coffee, he grabbed the bowl of oatmeal and walked down the hall to the basement, unlocking the door. Lying on the bed, chained by her wrist, was someone he didn't expect to bring back, but she kept pushing and threatened to expose his work.

Flashback night of the party.

"I have a variety of women," Neal muttered over the phone. He stood in Governor Snyder's office on the phone.

"The girls should come clean and tested."

Neal grabbed a pen off the desk, pulling out the documents for transportation for bringing in more girls that can go unnoticed without coming back to his name.

"We have transportation confirmed."

Sending an email, Neal closed out of the computer and ended the call. The door pushed open with Missy shutting it behind her.

"Can I help you, Missy?"

"I heard you on the phone."

"I don't know what you're talking about."

"Neal, I'm not stupid." Missy stumbled to the chair, holding a bottle of wine in her hand.

She lifted it to her lips.

"Maybe you should ease up on the wine."

"Maybe you should ease up on the hookers."

"Hookers."

"Yeah, I heard you talking about buying girls."

"Does Travis know your back here?"

Dropping the bottle on the floor, Missy crawled on top of the desk, crossing her legs.

"What are you doing?"

"I know you've been watching me."

"How old are you, Missy?"

Giggling, she ran her hand down his chest.

"Old enough to know that you're doing something bad."

Grasping her wrist, he twisted it back.

"Ouch... let me go."

"Bitch, you have no idea what I'm capable of doing."

"I'm sorry."

"You're going to be."

Present.

Turning the light on in the room, Neal moved her hair out of her face, running the back of his palm across her cheek. He watched as she winced over the black eye he gave her.

"You should have kept your mouth shut."

"Please let me go home."

"You're going somewhere. Just not home."

"Travis is going to wonder where I am." Missy pushed his hand away.

"Eat."

"I'm not hungry."

"Eat or starve, it doesn't matter to me."

Putting the bowl down on the bed, Neal looked around at the scattered clothes of her dress and shoes.

"I'm moving you out of here today."

"Please, I won't say anything."

"I don't believe you." He went to the door as she threw a bowl of oatmeal against the wall.

"I'm off to work."

Jogging up the stairs, Neal grabbed his coat and keys, placed his wallet in his pants pockets, and reset the alarm, leaving his house and getting in the town car. Heading to the governor's office, Neal checked over the latest poll numbers for re-election in the next few months.

FIFTEEN MINUTES LATER, the security detail opened the door, letting him out of the car. He shook hands with a few coworkers outside. Seeing his secretary at her desk, she held out messages he needed to return. Unlocking his door and removing his coat, Neal stood at the window, seeing his driver talking with a few men.

"You're early."

"I have a meeting with Travis."

"Do you want coffee?"

"Yeah, with a little rum."

"This early?"

"When do you question me so much, Olivia?"

"No reason, Mr. Kenan."

Ring! Ring!

"Kenan."

"Come to my office," Snyder said.

"Yes, sir, Governor."

Neal grimaced, scratching his chin.

"Here's your coffee."

"I don't want it."

Stalking to the governor's office, he heard yelling outside of his closed door. Knocking, he pushed the door open.

"Do you have any idea how much money I'm losing?" Travis asked.

"Governor, what's the problem?"

"These numbers are the problem. I might actually have a challenger."

Snyder tossed the newspaper on the desk.

"You shouldn't stress about early numbers."

"What the hell is happening with the damn murder of those girls?"

"I'm handling it, Governor."

"I doubt that; my numbers would look better than what the polls show."

"The public doesn't feel safe with the murders."

"Where are you with that anyway?"

"The mayor has the chief of police working twenty-four-seven on the case."

"I want someone arrested for this ASAP, Neal!"

"We both do, sir."

Standing from his chair, Governor Snyder grunted and paced in front of his chair.

"I haven't heard from Missy."

"Did you have a fight?"

"Juliette caught us going into my office the other night at the party."

"Governor."

"Last thing I need is a lecture from you."

"She's probably just ignoring your calls."

"You think so?"

"She's young. Give it a day or two."

"It's not like her to ignore my calls."

"Take your wife out to dinner and try being a husband."

"Juliette's not talking to me right now either."

"We need the public to believe you're a family man."

"Yeah, family man," Snyder groaned, rubbing the back of his neck.

"Anything else?"

Governor Snyder pulled his cell phone out of his pocket, scrolling over photos of Missy and him together. Motioning his hand that he didn't need anything else.

"Great, I'll be in my office." Neal turned, leaving Governor Snyder's office and taking his phone out of his pocket to send a text message to his security at home.

Neal: Take care of our guest.

Jimmy: Same place?

Neal: See how much she's worth.

"Mr. Kenan, I have Mayor Henton on line one," his assistant said.

"Thanks, Olivia." Neal closed out of his messages and picked up the receiver from the edge of the desk.

"Mayor Henton."

"Neal, I'm surprised to hear from you."

"Well, I do work on behalf of the governor."

"Is everything okay?"

"That's why I'm calling."

"We don't have any updates on the murders."

"Hummm... Did you see the numbers for Governor Snyder re-election?"

"Not lately."

"Get this case wrapped up now, or you'll find yourself out of a job."

"Is that a threat?"

"I don't make threats, Mayor." Neal heard the end of the dial tone, holding the phone in his hand.

ADAM ORDERED a glass of white wine as he sat in Longhorn Steakhouse, watching Patricia swish over to his table. He smiled as he stood to hug her and pull the chair out for her to sit. Taking her black shawl off her shoulders, Patricia smiled back.

"You look just as lovely as at the dinner."

"Thank you, Adam."

Their waitress came to the table holding a glass of water.

"Welcome to Longhorn. I'm Joanne," she said.

"Can we get another glass of white wine for my guest?"

"Sure, anything to eat?" Joanne asked.

"No, thank you," Patricia said.

"Are you sure? They have great buffalo burgers."

"Positive. I'm here for business, remember."

"I'll bring your wine right out." Joanne took her menu, strolling back to the kitchen. Longhorn opened two years ago in Camden to bring jobs back to the town and increase tourism.

"Something about you, Patricia."

"Adam, let me be clear. We're here to talk business."

"What about after we conclude our business?"

Gripping the glass of water, Patricia smirked, taking a sip.

"I won't be here for long."

"That breaks my heart."

"I've been known for breaking hearts and more."

"I might like that." Adam reached over the table to touch her hand.

She slid her hand away.

"My business, as I told you, deals in investments."

"Straight to business, huh?"

She tilted her head to the side.

"What do you have for me?"

Looking around the restaurant, it was mostly empty except for one or two couples engaged in conversation. Joanne came back from the kitchen, passing her glass of wine to her.

"Thank you," Patricia told me.

"I can't give you the exact details. Gotta protect myself, you know."

"Then why are we here?" she questioned.

"Some of my investments deal with importing and transporting."

"Like shipping ports?"

"Something like that."

Sitting back in her chair, Teagan stared into Adam's eyes, wondering what shipping ports had to do with the dead girls at the farm. Preparing to ask him a question, her phone interrupted.

"Sorry, I need to take this." Teagan opened her purse to grab her ringing phone.

"Do you need privacy?"

"If you don't mind."

"No problem. I have to use the little boy's room." Adam stood from his seat, buttoning his jacket and heading to the bathroom.

"Talk to me."

"Have you seen the news?" Spider asked.

"No, why?"

"We have another problem."

"What's wrong?"

"Once again, The Firm is getting the limelight we didn't want."

As she spoke with Spider, her phone clicked over with another call.

"I have another call, Spider. Hold on."

"Sure."

"Hello."

"Teagan, you need to come back home," Christian said.

"Christian? What's the matter?"

"I just received a call from our lawyer; you need to appear before the Senate," Christian said.

"The Senate."

"Everything okay?" Adam questioned, his hand on her shoulder.

"Who's that?" Christian asked.

So much going on, Teagan couldn't think straight as a migraine formed.

"Christian, let me call you back." Teagan hung up and, grabbing her purse, she jumped up, running out of the restaurant.

"Patricia! Hold up!" Adam called out, running behind her.

Jumping in the awaiting car with Spider driving, she ignored Adam.

"When can I see you again?" he yelled.

"Go!" Teagan shouted at Spider.

"The guys are packing up now."

Logging into social media, Teagan read all of the reports, removing the wipes in her purse to clean off her makeup. Tossing the wig into the backseat, she slid out of her heels and into her tennis shoes.

"Do you think this has to do with the case?"

"I can bet my last dollar it does."

"I agree; we're getting too close."

"The guys are meeting us at the airport to fly to DC."

"Has the president contacted you?"

"No, I assumed he didn't want to make it seem like he's somehow interfering."

"That makes sense."

"How long before we get to the airport?"

"About thirty minutes."

"Adam was talking about importing and transporting."

"What does that mean?"

"Your guess is as good as mine."

"This damn town has more secrets than Washington."

"At least in Washington, you know who's stabbing you in the back."

EIGHT

Morning in DC.

"Have a seat," President Sanders said.

"Thank you, sir."

"I have to say this doesn't get easier."

"No, it doesn't."

"How's the case going?" President Sanders questioned.

"Slow." Teagan clasped her hands together.

"Tell me the truth, are we going to make an arrest?"

"Honestly, I don't know. This seems to be more than one person."

"I agree with Agent Stone, sir," Spider commented.

"Agent Stone, your face has become the front and center of The Firm."

"I know."

"The Agency was built to weed out people who are trying to bring down our country's value."

"Yes, sir."

"Along the way, you've had to constantly fight adversaries not only foreign, but domestic."

"What are you saying, sir?"

"Maybe it's time we saw this as an opportunity to end The Firm."

This was the moment she'd been hoping for when they brought her back in to go undercover, and now she didn't know how to feel. Knocking on the door, she entered with the chief of staff and Secretary Kelton.

"Mr. President, you have another meeting," he said.

"Thanks, Teagan. Go answer the questions, this shouldn't last long," President Sanders spoke. Teagan and Spider nodded, shaking hands with President Sanders, treading out of his office, and passing Kelton.

THE FIRM'S LAWYER, flanked by Teagan and the rest of her team, marched into the room, looking around at all the reporters and senators talking amongst themselves.

"I see they decided to make this live," Spider whispered.

"Senator is looking to put on a show."

"Don't worry, she's just looking to score political points," Gary said.

"How many times have you done this, Gary?" Teagan asked.

"Too many to count." He placed his briefcase on the table, removing files.

Gregory, Daughtrey, Broderick, and Spider all sat behind Teagan as Senator Steinman called for everyone to enter and take a seat.

"What if something is classified?" Teagan asked.

"She knows certain things are classified."

"She's been on all the news circuits talking about taking us down," Daughtrey said.

"Gregory, look into her," Teagan whispered, leaning back in her seat.

He threw a thumbs up.

"We're going to begin in five minutes," Steinman said.

"Is there anything I need to know before we begin?" Gary inquired.

"You know everything we've done is by the book."

"What about the things that aren't in the book?"

"I suggest you keep it from coming up." Teagan licked her lips, sat forward, and poured a glass of water.

"Please raise your right hand," Senator Steinman told Teagan, standing in front of the cameras and congressmen over the defense budget committee and promising to tell the truth and explain in front of the world what The Firm was all about. Her attorney requested a closed meeting, but Steinman was firm on pushing her own agenda and wanted to make an example out of the team.

"Agent Stone, you are here to tell the truth."

"I am."

"Take a seat, please."

"Before we get started, I request one more time to keep the cameras out of this meeting," Gary told them.

"Request denied, Mr. Rogers," Steinman spoke.

The room went silent.

"Senator Palmer, you have the first question."

"Thank you, Senator. Agent Stone, you're married with three children, correct?"

"Yes."

"Does your family know what you do for a living?" Palmer asked.

"What relevance does this line of questioning have to do with my client?" Gary argued.

"Trying to gain clarity on Agent Stone's life."

"I agree with that question. Are you disagreeing with Mr. Rogers?" Steinman spoke up.

Holding his hand over the microphone, he whispered to Teagan, "What do you think?"

"It's fine. I know what they're doing. I'm used to interrogations."

"Go ahead, Senator."

"As I stated, Agent Stone, does your entire family know of your work?" Palmer asked.

"My family knows I work for the government."

"You're a spy, isn't that true?" The clicking of cameras and rumbling from reporters were shocking as they scrambled to get Teagan's facial reactions.

"Retired SEAL, sir."

"What about the reports of Deputy Brooks?" Steinman brought up, passing a sheet of paper over to another senator.

"Classified."

"You're under oath, Agent Stone," Steinman remarked.

"Senator, I put my life on the line, along with my men, to protect the country."

"We have no doubt you want to protect the country, but some of your techniques are questionable," Steinman said.

"I disagree."

"The files from The Firm start back from the Iraq War," Steinman said.

"What relevance, Senator?" Gary asked.

"How many people have you killed, Agent Stone?"

"My client will not answer that," Gary interrupted.

"How about we take a five-minute break," Steinman said.

An aide approached and whispered in her ear. Taking another sip of water, Teagan looked over her shoulder at her team.

"How long do we have to do this?" Teagan asked Gary.

"Depends on the next few minutes."

"Gregory, head out and see what you can come up with, Spider, stay investigating the case."

"Are you sure?" Spider replied.

"Yeah, I'm not giving up this case."

"We'll now continue if your client is ready, Mr. Rogers," Martha said.

"We're ready, Senator," Gary spoke.

"Great, Senator Gilmone, you have the next question," Martha informed.

"Thank you. Agent Stone, I understand you're overseeing a case in Nebraska." Gilmone leaned into the microphone.

"It's an ongoing case I can't talk about."

"I understand, but how do you approach these cases in general?" Gilmone inquired.

"Everything comes from the president."

The room erupted in conversation. Steinman hit the gavel to quiet the room.

"You're located out of the Pentagon, correct?"

"The main office was moved to the Pentagon, but we work out of the New York branch."

"The funding over the years has increased, but the amount of information has decreased," Gilmone implied.

"If that's your impression..." Teagan answered.

"Agent Stone, do you think this is a game? I can assure you that we take this hearing seriously."

"I would never presume you'd take this as a joke, Senator."

"Gilmone, continue," Martha insisted.

"Agent Stone, we noted that you were missing for a few years between working at The Firm."

"Is that a question?" Teagan asked.

Senator Gilmone cleared his throat. "That is a question."

"I needed a break."

"A break, or did you lose your memory?" Gilmone questioned, smirking as the cameras flashed in front of her eyes.

"Senator, I'd like to request a recess," Gary asked.

"I think today was enough, and we can end the line of questioning," Martha informed.

Teagan stood with her attorney as everyone piled out of the room, and reporters shoved cameras in her face, trying to get a scoop.

"Agent Stone! Agent Stone!"

Running toward her car, she slid in with Broderick and Daughtrey behind her and Gary getting in the front seat as the door closed.

"That old bitch is trying to bring you down," Daughtrey muttered.

"Gary, I don't want my family involved."

"I'll make some calls," Gary replied.

"How long do we have to be here?" Broderick questioned.

"Maybe a few days."

"We have a case, and then we just happen to get pulled into a senate hearing," Teagan argued.

"I agree this seems suspect, but let it play out," Gary answered as the car drove off.

"Did you get anything from that Adam guy?" Daughtrey wondered.

"Not really but look into him more and get some intel on Steinman."

AN HOUR LATER, Teagan arrived back at the hotel in DC that The Firm was paying for while she went through the hearing. Walking out of the shower in a white robe, she sat on the bed and opened her laptop, scrolling through emails and messages. They weren't any closer to finding the killer, and more girls came up missing. While en route to her hotel, she got a message from Spider that a woman named Missy came up missing. She looked at the photo of the girl lying in a dumpster with her hands tied with rope and remembered she was the woman Governor Snyder was talking to at the dinner party.

"How long ago was she found?" Teagan asked.

"The coroner is still on the scene; no definite answers," Spider responded.

"They're getting sloppy."

"The governor's pissed."

"Surprised he isn't elated that his secret isn't out."

"He did a press conference talking about how she worked on his campaign."

"Ugh..." Teagan fell back on the bed, holding the phone to her ear.

"Find out everything we can about his staff."

"Should we head back to Camden?"

"Yeah, but I need to see my family first."

"How about you spend time with the family and then come meet us back down there," Spider suggested.

"You're right."

"Get some sleep, T."

"Thanks, you too."

Teagan hung up and tossed the phone on the bed, staring at the ceiling.

"Importing and transporting," she mumbled to herself.

NINE

The next morning in DC, Teagan headed to the airport to fly out to New York, letting Gary handle the hearing. Taking a cab, she jumped out, grabbed her bags, and headed through the terminal when her cell phone went off.

"Agent Stone."

"Agent Stone, this is Mayor Henton."

"Mr. Henton, what can I do for you?" Checking in at the gate, she scanned her ID and loaded her bags with the attendant.

"I wanted to call to see if any new updates have happened."

"I'm afraid I've been a little slammed with Washington."

"I did hear about some investigation and you being out there to testify."

"That's true, and my lawyer is continuing with the hearing."

"Will this hinder you finding the person?"

"No, as a matter of fact, I sent my people back to Camden."

"Great, when are you coming?"

"In a few days, I need to go to New York first."

"I just want to make sure we can give the families resolution."

"Mayor, I have to board the plane, but we'll find out who's behind the killings."

"Thank you, Agent Stone."

"See you soon."

"Boarding New York Flight 345."

TWO DAYS LATER, New York afternoon.

Teagan and Christian watched as the kids played with water guns, running around the backyard with their friends. They invited family and friends for a fun afternoon of a barbeque and card games. Christian went to the store and got food for the grill, and she estimated that a day or two with her family would satisfy before she headed back to Camden on the case. More girls were going missing, and the governor was getting more pissed off with talking to reporters.

"It turned out good, right?" Christian flipped the burgers over on the grill as Teagan passed him a beer.

"The kids are having fun."

Christian glanced at the laughing kids scattered around the yard. They'd recently had it expanded to include a deck for the pool, canopy sitting area, and the garden cut down. Tegan's mom picked up Tatum in her arms.

"She's getting big, Mom! Put her down," Teagan yelled.

She waved Teagan off.

"Tell me about the hearings."

"Not today, Christian. CJ, come and eat!"

"Teagan, we need to talk about this. It affects the kids."

"Don't you think I know that?"

Teagan unwrapped the potato salad, making a plate for CJ as he stomped over mad that he had to stop playing.

"What's with the long face?" she asked, adding a hamburger and fries.

"I'm not hungry, Mommy."

"You barely ate breakfast."

"Can I play a little longer?" he questioned.

"When you're done eating." She handed the plate over with a napkin, taking the gun out of his hands.

"Aghhh...." CJ blew out a breath of frustration.

She rubbed the top of his head.

"Stop fussing and eat."

"Yes, ma'am."

"Teagan, you could go to jail, do you understand that?" Christian slammed the tongs down on the grill.

Teagan rolled her eyes, looking around the backyard, closing the space between her and Christian.

"Calm down."

"You don't care, do you?"

Relaxing her shoulder, she peered into his eyes, seeing the worry and stress. Reaching up, she placed her hands on both sides of his face.

"I promise, I'm not going anywhere."

Wrapping his arm around her back, he pulled her in close, pecking her on the lips.

"Ewww, gross, Daddy," CJ said, holding his plate up for more food.

"I thought you weren't hungry?" Teagan asked.

"Hard work catching my victims."

Teagan froze at his statement.

"Teagan," Christian called her name.

"Huh.."

"You all right? You blacked out on me."

"Ummm, yeah... I'll be right back." Teagan headed into the house, but Christian gripped her hand.

"You said no work today; it's Saturday."

Smiling, she kissed him again on the lips.

"Won't be long at all."

Running inside, she went to her office, taking out Adam's business card from her bag.

Debating on calling, she thought of a plan to get him on the phone since she left him without any explanation.

Picking up the office phone, she dialed Spider instead.

"Teagan, we're a little busy."

"What's going on?"

"At the medical examiner's office getting the file on Missy."

"Any new information?"

"She had a slit throat; died within a few hours."

"The other victims were killed slowly, methodically."

"You're thinking of two different people."

"Yeah or whoever did this was in a hurry."

"When are you coming here?"

"Hopefully in the next day or two."

"Is the family's good?"

"Yes, besides Christian being worried about the senate hearing."

"Really can't blame him."

"I know. Let me call you back. I need to check in with Gary."

"See you soon."

"You too," Teagan said, ending the call. Glancing outside at the family, she typed in the president's number.

"Teagan, we never talked this much before."

"I need you to make this go away."

He sighed.

"Give me a minute, Meghan," the president said.

"Yes, Mr. President."

"You know if I interfere, that will make it even worse."

Taking a seat in her chair, Teagan said, "Mr. President, I understand what you're saying, but we might be dealing with two killers."

"Wait a minute."

"I have a feeling it's one and a copycat."

"Have you spoken with the chief about this new evidence?"

"No, I want to keep it under wraps."

"You're not thinking the chief of police is behind these killings."

"Honestly, it could be the entire town."

"Teagan, The Firm is the best in these types of situations. Are you saying the FBI should take over the case?"

"No, what I'm saying is that Senator Steinman, like Brooks, Diablo, and everyone else, is bullshitting me!" she shouted.

"Feel better?"

"I apologize, Mr. President."

"Maybe you should hand the case over and take some time with your family or go talk with someone."

"I don't need a shrink."

"Talking to a therapist can help get your thoughts together."

"Do you talk to a therapist?"

"Classified."

She chuckled at his answer.

"Thank you, Mr. President."

"I'll see what I can do about the hearing."

"Yes, sir."

Dialing Adam's number, she watched Christian run after CJ and Cole with the water gun through the window.

"Adam Gardner."

Sitting back in her seat, she introduced herself, "Mr. Gardner, this is Patricia Langston."

"Well, to what do I owe the pleasure of this phone call?"

"I wanted to apologize to you for leaving so suddenly."

"Does that mean you'll have dinner with me?" he asked.

Laughter from the kids grew close to her office door.

"When I'm back in town, but that depends on if you can give me a little more information."

"At dinner."

Gripping the phone tighter, she bit her bottom lip.

"You drive a hard bargain, sir."

"You're a beautiful one, Patricia."

"I bet you say that to every woman."

A knock at her door startled her.

"Only the ones I see potential in."

"Mommy!"

"Who's that?" he questioned.

"TV. Sorry, let me call you back." She hurriedly hung up the phone.

"Mommy, can we have some ice cream?" Tatum questioned, with Cole next to her.

"Did you both eat?" Teagan walked from around her desk, tossing the business card in the trash can.

"I did!" Tatum said.

"Sure, only one of each." Teagan gripped their hands, walking into the kitchen. For the rest of the afternoon, she enjoyed the laughter and comfort of her family all together.

Later that night, after cleaning up and putting the kids to bed, she poured her favorite bath soap in the tub, grabbed a book, and relaxed with soft music while the whole house was asleep.

TEN

"Watch where you're going!" a guy in a red truck yelled. Teagan honked her horn as she drove the kids to school. Sunday dinner with Christian's parents brought back the simple times when she didn't have the world looking at her every move.

"Mom, can you sign this?" Cole asked.

"What's this?" Teagan picked up the form from his teacher.

"Field trip," Cole replied.

"You're just now giving me this, Cole?"

Teagan grabbed the pen out of his hand, signing her name.

"I forgot."

"Uhm... huh."

"Thanks, Mommy." Cole opened the door.

"Can I get a kiss?"

"No, I'm too old for that." Cole looked around at his classmates.

"Really, Cole?"

"Mom, that's for babies."

"You're my baby."

"Oh, My God!" Cole leaned in the car and kissed her fast on the cheek before anyone saw her, covering his face with the sheet of paper.

"I thought Tatum was dramatic!" Teagan blurted out.

Cole waved her off, and she laughed, pulling into traffic toward the office. She sipped on her coffee, listening to more of the hearings on the radio.

"These agencies only protect the powerful. We need transparency," Martha said

"President Sanders is not above the law," Gilmone said.

Turning the radio off, she shook her head, pulled in the garage, and held her badge out for the security guard.

"Clear, Director." The guard allowed entry.

"Thanks," Teagan replied, driving in and parking in her usual spot.

"I thought you would've taken today off." Spider met her at the elevator.

"You're here early."

"I slept here."

"You need to go home, Spider."

"I showered and ate breakfast."

"We have to have a life outside of this place." Teagan waved her hand around the elevator, hitting the button to her floor.

"This case is just pissing me off."

"Same."

"I talked with the chief again, and he's hearing it from the governor just as much as we are."

"What did the chief say?"

"Nothing really new, but he offered to put in a curfew for the town."

"It'll take more than a curfew." Teagan and Spider

stepped off the elevator, heading to her office. Unlocking her door, she hung her coat on the rack and dropped her bag on the top of the desk.

"What did the president say about the hearings?"

"Nothing yet; he's trying to work on Steinman."

"She has it out for you."

Teagan sat at her desk, picking up her messages.

"Which is strange because we've never crossed paths."

She kicked her feet up on the desk.

"Most of the people are enemies of President Sanders."

"Exactly, so why don't they go after him and not me?"

"Because it's easier to cut the minions down, then the king will fall."

She held the messages up to her chin, staring at Spider.

"What do we know right now?"

"Girls are going missing, ending up dead."

"All killed at different times but located at the same place."

"The person knows the town and is familiar with the area."

"It has to be someone in public office; they trust the people."

"Either that or drugged."

"Did Gregory make any headway?"

"Not yet; he's just as torn up about these cases."

"Damn."

"Well, meet me at the shooting range. I need to let off some steam."

HOURS LATER, Teagan arrived home with the kids, holding bags of groceries; Christian was lying across the couch when Tatum ran up and plopped down on his legs.

"When did you get here?" Teagan asked.

"About an hour ago." Christian moved Tatum, stood, and grabbed the bag out of Teagan's hand, kissing her on the lips. Throwing her purse on the couch, she followed him in the kitchen.

"How was work?"

"It was good. What about you?" he asked.

"Fine, quiet."

"Any news on the senate hearings?"

"No, but the president said he's working on trying to get it wrapped up."

"Why don't you relax, and I'll get dinner ready for tonight."

"Are you sure?"

"Yep, you've been nonstop since coming back."

"Thanks, honey. I'm going to shower and change."

"Okay, tell the kids to do their homework."

"Yes, boss," she chortled.

Running away before Christian could catch up, Teagan ran to the boys' room and knocked on the door.

"Come in!" Cole shouted.

"Honey, start on your homework."

"Okay."

"Now, Cole. Put the game away."

"Yes, ma'am."

Teagan went to the bedroom and turned on the TV as she grabbed some clothes from her drawer to change into.

"I'm voting to keep torture techniques by The Firm criminal," Martha said on the news segment.

"Are you saying the president condones torture, Senator Steinman?" the reporter asked.

"The president knows what he's doing with this program," Martha answered.

"This woman is crazy."

Shaking her head, she walked into the bathroom, turned the water on, and picked up her shower cap.

"Babe, you want tacos tonight?" Christian asked from the bedroom door.

"That's fine."

"What are you watching?"

"That crazy senator is on the news talking about the president condoning torture."

"Seriously?"

"Yeah."

She opened the cabinet to grab a clean towel when the house phone rang.

"It's probably for you." Christian headed back to the kitchen.

"I won't be long." Teagan turned the shower off, ran back in, and picked up the phone.

"Hello."

"I tried calling your cell, but no answer," President Sanders said.

"It's in my purse. I had it on silent while I was at work."

"Senator Steinman is out for blood."

"I see."

"A few things are moving on my end, so be prepared to get the word on flying out to Nebraska."

"You still want us to handle the case?"

"I refuse to let her win."

"Yes, Mr. President."

"Good. Enjoy the rest of your night, and I'll be in touch."

"You as well, Mr. President."

ELEVEN

Flashback

The low opera music played in the background. At the same time, Audrey stood in the corner, sipping on a glass of champagne and watching as Secretary Todd Kelton talked with other congressmen at the annual mayor's meeting in Nebraska at the governor's mansion. She hated coming to these boring events because Mayor Henton always got wrapped into some type of savior complex and tried to win over his father's respect. She'd worked for the father, even sleeping with him behind his son's back, and was promised once things transitioned to his son as mayor, her position as secretary would stay the same. She made her hours, took lunch when she felt like it, and knew she wouldn't be fired because of her connection to the longtime Henton name. As a matter of fact, she met the father when she was only seventeen years old when he spoke at her high school. Gaining an internship was an opportunity for her to get out of her mother's shadow, who only used her to get what she wanted. Working at his office helped her learn the ropes of politics as his assistant. Late nights turned into more than just flirting.

Audrey thought she was in love with Henton's father. When she learned he would never leave his wife, Audrey decided she was only out for herself and making money by doing what she did best— gaining the upper hand. Learning about the men who loved young girls in town, all the way up to Washington, benefited her in building a business. Now at thirty-two, she made it her priority while stalking her next client as they both kept making eye contact throughout the night. Lloyd was gullible and easy to manipulate like his father, so she whispered in his ear to find her another glass of champagne in order to get a few minutes alone.

"This is your last one for the night," Lloyd spoke, holding up the glass as he walked off.

Audrey smiled, holding two fingers crossed in the air, knowing she didn't care what he said. Dropping the smile once his back was toward her, Audrey fluffed her long hair out and pulled her sleeves lower, showing more cleavage, while strolling over to the window where Todd Kelton was laughing with Mayor Collins of Boston.

"I'm telling you, Andrew, Seattle might have a chance at the playoffs," Todd argued.

"Thanks for the confidence boost," Mayor Collins replied.

Stepping next to both men, Audrey grinned as they finished shaking hands.

"Mr. Collins, you have an urgent call," his assistant stated.

"Excuse me; I have to take this," Andrew informed me.

Todd nodded in agreement, sliding his hand in his inside jacket pocket, pulling out a cigarette case.

"I didn't know you could smoke here," Audrey said.

"You can't. I was heading outside."

"Do you mind if I join you?" Audrey asked.

"Why would a beautiful woman like you want to be around such an ugly habit," he flirted.

"Not all habits are ugly, sir."

"The ones I like are," he replied.

Letting her lead the way out front of the mansion, she walked through the crowd, dodging Llyod from finding out she was with Kelton.

"I see you're here with Henton's son." Todd lit his cigarette, blowing out smoke.

"I'm his secretary."

Todd held the silver case full of cigarettes up, offering her one.

"Thank you." She placed it between her lips, lighting it as she closed her eyes, taking in the first drag of the cigarette.

"You like working for Henton's family?"

"It has its perks."

"How old are you?"

"How old do you need me to be?"

Kelton smirked at her response.

"Something about you intrigues me."

"Good."

"I'm only here until tomorrow. Then, I fly out to Washington."

"That's fine."

"I have a hotel room."

"Following your lead, Mr. Kelton." She reached out, placing a hand on his chest.

"What about your boss?"

"He'll be fine."

AUDREY SLID her feet in her high heels two hours later as Secretary Kelton lay in bed, wrapped around a comforter and sheets.

"How much do you charge?" he questioned.

"For you, it was free," she said.

"You do this often."

"Do what?"

"Sleep with men in power?" he questioned.

She turned her back toward him to zip up her dress.

"The real question is why men sleep with women when they know they are married."

"What gave me away? I wasn't wearing my ring."

"I research my clients."

He chuckled to himself.

"So this is your business at night; during the day you work as a secretary?"

"Something like that."

"How many girls work for you?"

"Depends."

"On what?"

"If we're talking off the record, Mr. Kelton, I'm not in the business to end up in jail."

Kelton moved the comforter back, stood, and grabbed his pants, sliding one leg, then the other.

"I'm not a bad person."

"I hear that a lot." She leaned down, picking up her purse.

"Sometimes I like to relax with a young woman."

She smirked, knowing he was on track to being one of her clients.

"That can be arranged." Audrey cupped his chin, then turned and strolled to the door of the hotel room.

"Audrey," he called out.

Her hand gripped the door.

"I hope you understand this needs to be kept between us."

"Discretion is my middle name, Secretary Kelton."

PRESENT.

A few days later, Audrey pulled her shades off while sitting in her car, as she watched some high school girls talking in front of a local diner with some boys. Lighting up another cigarette, she thought of a way to get one of them in her car. Checking herself out in the mirror, Audrey peered as the two girls got into their car, leaving the boys alone. Following at a close distance, Audrey checked the time on her cell, noting her lunch break was almost up. Ten minutes later, the young blond girl dropped her friend off in front of an apartment building, then drove off. The blond, green-eyed cheerleader stopped at a stop sign, music blasting. Audrey took this as an opportunity to take advantage. Speeding up, Audrey hit her car from the back, causing them both to pull over to the side of the street. Dumping her cigarette, Audrey pulled her ID out of her purse and opened the door, putting on a wide smile as she approached. Knocking on her window, the young girl stepped out of the car looking annoyed.

"I'm so sorry; I wasn't paying attention," Audrey said.

"My dad's going to be pissed," the young girl said.

"Maybe he doesn't need to know."

"What do you mean?"

"I know a car guy who can fix your car without them knowing."

"I don't know."

"Listen, you, don't have to worry. It will probably take an hour or two."

"How can I get the car there?"

"You can ride with me to the shop, and I'll have it towed."

The young girl looked over at Audrey's car.

"How far is the shop? Maybe I can call my dad."

"You want him to know what happened to his car and end up getting in more trouble?"

"I guess you're right."

"It won't take long, probably about a five-minute drive."

Audrey led the girl over to the car.

"What's your name?"

"Emily. What's yours?"

Audrey dropped her pack of cigarettes on the floor in the front passenger seat.

"Teresa, shit! Can you grab my cigarettes from the floor?"

Emily buckled her seatbelt and bent down, grabbing the case.

"This won't hurt too much," Audrey said, sticking a needle in Emily's neck.

"Ouch... What is—" Emily muttered as her eyes drew low, falling back against the window and passing out.

"Something to help you sleep."

"AS WE WATCH THE HEARINGS, we're reminded of our democracy as citizens," Charles Daniels, CGN News, reported.

"That's right, Charles. As voters, you can't imagine

what goes on behind the scenes," Rachel from CGN News reported from DC.

"We are on the fifth day of hearings with Senator Steinman setting final statements," Charles said.

"As senators, we have an obligation to make sure the American people are kept informed," Martha said.

"I'd like to call a final vote," Senator Vail asked.

Picking up the gavel, Steinman called for reporters to quiet down.

"This hearing will come to a vote."

Turning the TV down, Teagan stood in her kitchen, preparing to pick up her kids from school. Teagan grabbed her keys off the holder, heading to the front door. Sean stood at the Range Rover, waiting for word.

"I'm driving myself, Sean."

"I'll follow."

"That's not necessary."

"Director, you know I can't do that."

"Fine. I can't get rid of you."

Hopping in her car, Teagan reversed out of her drive-way, turning left at the light, with Sean right behind her as she headed down the street to the freeway. Turning the radio on, Teagan listened to music while driving, thinking of a vacation she finally wanted to take once the case was solved. Approaching her exit, she signaled to get over to jump off, easing in the line of cars waiting to pick up their children. Her Bluetooth rang.

"I'm with the kids, Spider."

"We had another one."

"What?"

"Yeah, I just got off the phone with chief."

"Damn."

"I know we have the hearing, but we need to get back to Nebraska soon."

Driving up further, Teagan saw her kids running toward her car.

"Send over the information." Teagan unlocked the car door, letting the kids get inside. Tatum jumped in the front seat, while CJ and Cole went to the back passenger seats.

"Mommy, can we stop for ice cream?" Tatum asked.

"We have ice cream at home. Spider, let me call you back," Teagan replied.

"Hi, Spider!" all three kids blurted out.

As Teagan ended the call, she received an alert with information on the latest victim.

"Sit back, Tatum."

Glancing at the window to see Sean still following, Teagan tried to keep it together and not get emotional about another young girl popping up dead. Making it back home, Teagan parked and turned the radio up, letting the kids out of the car.

"We have breaking news that senators voted down to get rid of The Firm."

"Tatum, you forgot your homework." Teagan grabbed her bookbag and treaded to the front door of her house. Almost tripping over CJ's shoes, she dropped Tatum's backpack at the door.

"Go change your clothes and start on your homework, please."

"Mom, can we play the game please?" CJ said.

"Once you finish your homework." Teagan kissed him on top of his head. Cole and Tatum came running into the living room, and Teagan pointed to Tatum's backpack near the door.

The front door opened, and Christian walked in

holding a briefcase and the mail. Dropping them on the table, he kissed Teagan on the lips. Teagan led him to the kitchen to talk.

"I heard on the radio that they are not closing the Agency.

"Yeah, but I have to fly back to Nebraska."

"What happened?"

"Another victim."

"How old this time?"

"Not sure, but I won't be long."

"Okay. Just be careful, babe."

TWELVE

Sitting at the conference table the next morning, Gregory continued scanning and researching the new photos and evidence that came through from the medical examiner. He was used to seeing dead bodies and blood, but something about a young girl's life being over so soon, he had a harder time handling these types of cases without going on a rampage. On another screen, he watched the senate vote and news reporters talking about what it could mean if the votes went another way. He logged in all of the audiotapes he listened to and scanned all of the car tags the night of the governor's dinner. A few seconds later, Daughtrey marched into the room holding a folder; Broderick held a bag of chips in his hands. Dropping the folder on the table, Daughtrey smiled, tapping on the top of the folder.

"What's this?"

"Where's Spider?" Daughtrey asked.

"Probably in his office."

"I got the toxicology report."

"And?"

"The Nebraska medical examiner missed the needle injections."

"What are you talking about?"

"I wanted to have our people look deeper into these cases."

"You think the chief was trying to cover up?" Broderick asked.

"Probably, but all the girls were injected in the same spot behind their neck to put them to sleep."

"We have to tell Teagan," Gregory said.

"That still keeps us blind to what's going on," Broderick mentioned.

As they continued talking, Gregory had Daughtrey listening to audio tapes.

"I think I can arrange that," a woman whispered into the phone.

"Wait a minute, play that back," Broderick said.

"What part?" Daughtrey said.

"Did you hear that muffled voice?"

Rewinding the tape, Gregory hit play.

"I think I can arrange that."

"It's going to take time to figure out who that voice matches."

"I wonder what she was talking about," Broderick said.

Picking up the phone, Gregory dialed Spider's office.

"He's coming down." Gregory sat back in his set, crossing his arms, taking in the photos of all the dead girls.

TURNING THE STOVE DOWN, Teagan moved the salad bowl over to the counter and cut up tomatoes and onions. Before she headed back to Nebraska, she made

Christian's favorite fish, asparagus, salad, and strawberry shortcake. Christian came into the kitchen, wrapped his right arm around Teagan, and picked up the red bottle of wine off the cellar stand. She grabbed the wine opener from the drawer and took two glasses down from the cabinet.

"One glass before you go."

"Mhmmm..."

"Come on. It's my favorite meal, so let's celebrate with wine."

"All right, one glass. Are the kids still playing?"

"Yeah. I'll go get them to freshen up before dinner."

She tossed the salad together, plating it in a large white bowl. Teagan licked her finger, tasting the special sauce she made. Sliding on her gloves, she plated the fish and asparagus with loaves of bread. Wiping her hands clean, she tasted the piece of fish, when the phone rang. Christian gathered the kids into their seats from the backyard.

"Hello."

"Sorry to interrupt dinner."

"What's going on?"

"You should come in before we head to Nebraska."

"I just got the kids ready for dinner."

"Sorry, Teagan, but this can't wait."

"I'll be there as soon as I can." Hanging up the phone, Teagan went back into the kitchen smiling, then helped to make plates for the kids. Popping the cork on the wine bottle, he poured a glass for her and then himself.

"Ohh, can I have some wine?"

"No," Tegan and Christian said at the same time.

Both boys laughed at her.

"You're too young," CJ said.

"So! I can get what I want!" Tatum yelled.

"What did you say?" Teagan questioned.

"Huh."

"I can get what I want," Tatum said.

"You've been acting up lately, Tatum," Christian complained.

Teagan rose from her seat, thinking over those words. Picking up her cell phone, she dialed Spider's number.

"Are you on your way?"

"Not yet, but did we run all the police and city leaders through background checks?"

"I believe Gregory did," Spider muffled through the phone.

She heard him ask Gregory.

"He's running them again."

"From what we know, all the girls left with someone they trusted or felt comfortable around."

"Yeah."

"Dig deeper."

"Have you heard from the president about the outcome?"

"He's trusting we can solve this case; that's his priority."

"Hurry up, so we can."

"Is the plane ready?"

"Once you're here, we can get it loaded."

"Great, I'll be there soon."

Hanging up the phone, Teagan went down the hall to her office. She logged into her computer and checked the database of the Camden Police Department. Cole pushed her office door open, coming in with a bowl of strawberry shortcake and ice cream.

"What are you doing, Mom?"

Closing out the police files, she pulled up a chess game on the screen.

"Playing chess. Shouldn't you be eating dinner?"

"I did."

"Did you eat the asparagus?"

She patted her lap for him to sit.

"It was nasty."

He lifted a piece of cake for her to eat.

"It's healthy for you." She ate the cake, rubbing him on the back.

"You're leaving again tonight?"

"Yeah."

"I don't like your job."

"Me neither."

He grinned at her answer.

"Since you're the boss, can I be the second in command?"

"You want to become a SEAL?"

He shrugged his shoulders.

"I want to shoot guns."

"CJ, I do more than shoot guns."

"I like that part, though."

Laughing at his comment, she tapped him to get up.

"You're my son for sure."

"Can you teach me to shoot?"

"When you're eighteen."

"Shake my hand on the agreement."

"You don't trust me?"

"Mom, this is business."

"CJ, go shower for bed and give me that bowl."

Heading to put the bowl away, Teagan saw Christian sitting on the couch watching the re-airing of the senate hearing and Teagan's statement. Standing behind Christian, he grabbed her hand, kissing the back of her palm.

"You keep finding enemies."

"I guess I'm special."

"Special to me."

Teagan bent down, hugging him from behind.

"I'll see what the president says; this won't be the last attempt."

"That's what scares me."

THIRTEEN

The next morning.

Seeing the photos from Barton Restaurant, Teagan's upper lip scrunched into a scowl, knowing the public put these people in office to protect them. This type of betrayal would be crippling on the community and state. Todd Kenton, Neal Keenan, and Audrey all looked to be in an intense conversation. All this time, a woman helped kill young girls and feed lies to the public. Women like her disgusted Teagan, and she wanted to kill all three of them without a trial.

"What else do you have?" Teagan asked Gregory as they sat in the conference room.

"That Senator Steinman wasn't only behind these bogus hearings, but I have pictures of her with Todd in her office." Gregory scrolled through the pictures on the computer.

"How fast can we get to DC?"

"The private jet can have us there in less than an hour," Daughtrey answered.

"Get Henton on the line," Teagan said.

Rubbing her temples, she clenched her eyes closed, thinking of each way to torture and kill Audrey.

"Mayor Henton," he groggily answered.

Teagan stood and leaned against the phone in the center of the table.

"Mayor Henton, this is Agent Stone."

"Agent Stone, what's going on?"

"We know who's behind the deaths."

"Have you called the chief or Governor Snyder?"

"I'll let you handle that part."

"Mayor, I'm sending to your phone some photos we've received," Gregory explained.

"Pictures of what?" he asked.

Teagan looked from Broderick to Spider.

"Your secretary Audrey." He laughed at her revelation.

"It's true, Henton."

"You must have made a mistake; Audrey would never do anything like this."

She clipped her chin at Broderick, and he turned the recording on for Henton to listen.

"*I can't bring you anymore girls, Secretary,*" Audrey said.

"*The last girl was a mistake,*" Kelton said.

"*This puts me at a bigger risk; I need more money,*" Audrey replied.

"My God."

Broderick reached over and turned off the recording.

"Mr. Henton, I can't tell you how sensitive our time is to wrap this up."

"I understand."

"My team received information that the deal is going down in DC."

"We're sending you all the information that was collected."

"I'll have a statement sent out ASAP."

"Thank you, sir." Teagan ended the call.

"Next step is getting Senator Steinman to talk," Gregory mentioned.

"That shouldn't be hard."

Teagan walked toward the screen, with her back to the team, staring at the photos of the dock area with ships and cargo coming in and out.

"If we 're right, it should go down within the next forty-eight hours."

"Have you spoken with Sanders?" Broderick wondered.

"No, I'll call on our way to the Capitol."

"Suit up, boys." Spider said.

"Dead or alive?" Daughtrey asked.

Teagan turned around at the question.

"Hostile, then we take them down. Gregory, get coordinated with our people surrounding the area."

"How far of a range can we get?"

"At least six miles. Can we lock it down?"

"What about the Coast Guard?" Spider queried.

"I don't want to tip them off. Neal is counting on Kelton to have the cargo available."

"Maybe one of us can go in as security," Daughtrey said.

Rubbing her chin, Teagan thought about his suggestion.

"Gregory, can you make a fake ID ASAP?"

"Coming right up."

"Good. Daughtrey, you'll go in tonight. Broderick, you're running the transportation."

"You want me on surveillance?" Gregory asked.

"Yes, Spider and I will go in with Daughtrey and a few men," Teagan explained.

The entire team sat around the table as Spider called for more agents.

"This is Gage."

"Gage, this is Spider."

"What's going on? I don't get calls from the New York team often."

Gage Tate was a thirty-two-year-old single dad with a daughter he was raising with his parents. His wife was killed in an automobile accident years ago, and he'd taken on the role of leader of the DC Striker team. While Teagan ran the entire Agency, she hadn't worked alongside other members of The Firm until now. Going to DC, they would need more manpower; knowing Gage had the knowledge of the DC area would come in handy.

"A drop in is happening, and I need a tour guide," Spider said.

"I love tours." Gage chuckled.

"Good, this one could be rough. Are you up for that type of dance?"

"Brother, I love those rough dances."

"Will be in town soon, heading out to the plane once this call ends."

"What are we hunting for?"

"Trafficking."

"Son of a bitch!" Gage growled.

"You're a father, so you know how sensitive we have to be with this case."

"Yeah, man, who's behind this?"

"Check your phone after the call ends."

"See you soon." Gage hung up, not waiting for any more instructions.

"You think he'll be able to control himself?" Teagan asked.

"No," Spider answered, rising out of his seat.

"Perfect."

Teagan smirked, patting Spider on the back as she walked out of the room.

FORTY MINUTES LATER, standing outside the private airport, dialing the president's secure line, Teagan waited outside the plane as the team loaded cargo. She hadn't spoken to Christian since last night, but she promised herself once they arrived, she'd try to let him know she had made it safely before going on her mission.

"Agent Stone."

"Mr. President." Teagan sighed, feeling nervous about what she was going to explain.

"I saw you've made strides with the Nebraska case."

"Yes, sir. Even though the bogus hearing by Steinman was trying to distract us, we've made headway."

"Who's the suspect?"

"Secretary Todd Kelton."

The call went quiet.

"Do you have proof of this?"

"Unfortunately, I do."

He mumbled low.

"Is that the highest level of corruption?"

"As far as I can tell, sir, besides Steinman being used."

"She's always been a sparring partner, but not this devilish."

"I'm not sure if she knew he was trafficking girls, but we have to keep that to ourselves."

"What can I do to help?"

"My men are loading up now. We'll be in DC in the next hour; it's going on five in the afternoon now."

"You have the support of the police and whatever else you need."

"Thank you, sir, but I'd like to keep it to as few people as possible."

"Agent Stone?"

"Yes, sir."

"Be careful."

"Always, Mr. President."

Spider jogged up the steps of the plane.

"Locked and loaded!" Daughtrey called out, pounding on the back of the plane.

Grabbing a seat, Teagan looked out of the window as Sean drove off back to the office. Blowing out a breath, she closed her eyes briefly, placing the seatbelt on as everyone clamored for a seat.

"Daughtrey, check your email," Gregory said.

"Damn, that's fast," Daughtrey replied, pulling up his email from his phone.

"No doubt." Gregory and Daughtrey fist bumped.

"Did you send Gage all the information?" Teagan questioned.

"Uploading now, boss," Gregory answered.

"We'll be taking off shortly; please turn off all devices," the stewardess demanded.

The seatbelt light came on, and everyone got comfortable as the plane lined up on the runway. A few moments after takeoff, she brought out trays of drinks and snacks for the team as they turned on their electrical devices. Gregory muttered something underneath his breath.

"Interesting," Gregory said.

"Something new," Spider commented.

"I got the financial records of the port docks."

"Let me guess; Todd Kelton is an investor," Teagan remarked.

"Before joining the Sanders administration, he co-founded Arrowlane LTD to a profit of close to five hundred million dollars." Gregory turned his computer around for Teagan to see.

"Assholes are going to probably use this as a new way to transport women."

"We have to stop them now." Spider's face screwed into a hard glare.

"Tell Gage to have his people already scoping out the location once we land. But don't engage," Teagan said.

Gregory typed on his computer as Spider sent a text message. Surveillance video footage popped up on Gregory's computer from his email, and he clicked the video, seeing vans approaching the loading dock.

"Teagan, we might have a problem."

"What?"

"I have two vans approaching the port now."

"Can you get eyes on who the company belongs to?"

"No, I just see them less than a few feet from getting inside."

"Shit! I thought we'd have a little more time to get set up."

"Should we tell Gage?" Broderick questioned.

Tapping her finger against the chair in thought, all eyes trained on her, waiting to see what direction she would give.

"Teagan."

"I'm thinking."

"They just signed in and drove through the gate," Gregory said.

"What's the name of the company?"

"Washington Port Pipeline, more than likely fake," Gregory replied.

"Tell Gage to stand back and keep surveillance. No one moves in until we get there."

"What if girls are moved?" Broderick asked.

"Then we need to have them followed, but I want all parties caught."

"Too much to keep track of, Teagan," Spider said.

"Not if we can get the president to lock down all airports, buses, and trains."

Spider's eyes rose in shock.

"Gregory, I want eyes on these vans without contacting the owners. We can't tip Kelton off."

An hour later, the team piled in the waiting cars at the airport, Teagan, Gregory, and Spider in one van, while Broderick and Daughtrey were in another.

"Remember to keep the line of communication open; nobody goes in without my go-ahead. Understood."

"Understood!" everybody said at the same time. A fleet of ten black Range Rovers lined up, driving out of the airport when three broke off, carrying Teagan and a few men from the DC office heading to make one more stop.

SENATOR STEINMAN CLOSED down her computer for the day, feeling the ramifications from the media storm of the committee hearings. Grasping her keys and purse, Martha edged toward the door, preparing to open it when Teagan burst through.

"OMG! You scared me." Martha held a hand to her chest.

"Senator, what's the rush?" Teagan closed the door behind her.

"Wh... What are you doing here?" Martha glanced at her phone, wanting to call for help.

"You're under investigation for helping a child sex trafficker." Teagan held up a warrant.

"I have no idea what you're talking about."

Teagan marched over to her desk, turning Martha's computer back on when a password link popped up.

"What's your password?"

"Agent, you have no idea—"

"Save the speech for someone who cares. I have a cargo ship coming in with women and girls about to be sold."

"What does that have to do with me?" she asked.

"You're wasting my time!" Teagan shouted, pushing the papers off her desk.

"I don't know what you're talking about."

Jumping in her face, Teagan pointed a finger at her chest.

"Secretary Kelton is a part of a sex trafficking ring, and you helped him."

Martha's mouth opened slightly, shaking her head in disbelief.

"Do you know what you just said?"

"Charges will be brought against Secretary Kelton, the governor's campaign manager in Nebraska, and you if I don't get your help."

"The only thing I know is that he wanted me to shut down The Firm."

"Put your password in now."

Grasping her arm, Teagan shoved Martha toward her desk.

"Okay, okay."

Checking the time, it was going on six-thirty, and Spider sent a message update to hurry up.

"Here's the file." Martha moved to the side as Teagan stepped forward, reading over the documents on the screen.

"Kelton was spearheading to close The Firm and run for president?"

"He told me he was only in it for being president. I didn't know anything about women being sold," Martha said as tears pooled in her eyes.

"Gregory will need this information." Teagan searched around her computer for any other information, sending the data to Gregory to go over later.

Finally getting everything she needed, Teagan sent a text message to Spider.

Teagan: Have security come up.

Spider: On it.

"Can I go now?" Martha asked.

"Yes."

Martha stood and walked toward the door.

"But you're not going home," Teagan said behind her back as security guards opened the door.

"Wait a minute. I didn't do anything wrong."

"Ma'am, you have to come with us," a guard told her, grabbing her by the arm. She jerked away.

"Let me walk with some dignity."

FOURTEEN

Running out of the building and jumping back in the Range Rover, Teagan lifted the bulletproof vest and binoculars. Taking the automatic weapon from the back seat, Spider started the car, and they drove over to the dock port to meet up with Gage and his team.

"How far out are we?"

Tapping on the navigation device, Spider turned at the stoplight from the Capitol building and headed into traffic. Speeding up, Teagan checked her weapon was loaded and prepared her mindset for the next few minutes before going into battle.

"You're nervous," Spider said.

"Not Teagan." Gregory held his cell phone forward for Teagan to watch.

"He's actually there," Teagan murmured.

The screen showed Todd, Neal, and Audrey standing outside a maroon cargo ship with the name Arrowlane LTD across it.

"How many did they account for so far?" Teagan inquired.

Passing her a radio headset, Teagan checked the feedback.

"He counted at least fifteen, but there could be more since they got there late."

Driving through the underpass of the entrance, the lights were turned on as the sunset hit the dock. Parking near the other cars at the building entrance, Teagan stepped out of the car with Spider following, spotting Gage approaching with his men.

Holding out a palm for a shake, Spider went to each man to express a thank you for helping on this mission.

"Have they tried to bring the girls out yet?"

Daughtrey carried a flashlight and taser and wore a basic port uniform while allowing people to enter and leave.

"On the radar, I have heat picking up in the cargo. I think we have more than one," Gage said.

"He wouldn't be that stupid," Gregory commented.

"Sick people like this will do anything," Spider said.

Grabbing the mic, she spoke into the headset.

"Broderick, lock down the exits and entrances. We're going in now." Teagan motioned behind Gage.

"Where do you want us?" Gregory asked.

"Gage and you on the left, Spider behind me," Teagan said.

"Let's go!" Gage whistled, waving his hand in the air.

Tegan and Gage split up and went on opposite ends of the perimeter.

"Try not to give yourselves away."

Staying low, holding the gun up, Teagan wiped the sweat away as she continued walking to the end of the dock where Todd was located. Passing across to the next section, she was spotted, and a guard lifted his gun in her face, about to shoot. She held out her hand for the men to stop moving.

"Don't move," he said.

She pretended to surrender with her hands up in the air.

"Easy now, you don't want to do this."

"I need to radio this to my boss."

She lowered her left hand behind her back, letting them know on her count when to move.

"How much are they paying you?"

"Lady, keep your hands up!" he yelled as she eased in closer, cutting the distance between them. The agitation and nervousness let her know she was getting to him before he came unhinged and blew their cover. Soon as he looked to his left, she took the opportunity to pop him in the throat. He started choking, and she grabbed the gun, wrapping her arm around his throat and putting him to sleep.

"I got him," Gregory said, taking him behind the wall near the trash.

"We only have a few minutes before they notice he's gone."

Getting closer to the Arrowlane section, biting her bottom lip, Teagan looked behind, making sure the team was following.

"Ready?"

"Ready."

"On my count, one, two, three!" Teagan shouted and shot the security guards, watching Neal and Audrey duck low and try to run away.

"Grab them, Gregory." Teagan sent a shot in the head of another guard. Gregory crossed over and went down the corridor to the right and ran to catch up to Audrey and Neal.

"Bitch!" another hired gunman cursed, dropping his gun and trying to fight Teagan. Sending a headbutt, she growled and dropped the gun, grabbing the headpiece off her face. He tossed it on the ground as she kicked him in the side of the leg, and he grunted.

"Is that all you have for me?" He smirked, wiping the blood off his lip.

"Let's go, big boy." Teagan grinned, elbowing him in the stomach and punching him in the left jaw as they continued shooting around them.

"We're here to help." she heard Spider say as the whispers and cries rose.

"Ahhhh! You bitch!" Spider looked behind him and saw Teagan being choked and the security guard on top of her.

"Shit! Gage, get them out of here," Spider said.

Gregory caught up to Audrey as she tried to jump in the car with Neal and grabbed her by the hair.

"Please don't kill me," Audrey cried out.

Teagan twisted and turned while under the guard's weight, putting all her strength into pushing him off her. Across the way, Todd slipped out while Spider moved the women into the vans to get them to safety.

"Get me out of here!" Todd called out, holding money in his hands.

"Yes, sir," the fisherman replied.

Chaos erupted all over as helicopters from the news stations flew over the area, trying to get the scoop.

"Aghhh!" Teagan screamed, lifted her leg, and bucked her hip, throwing the guard off and triggering Teagan to get a heads up, poking him in the eye.

"Motherfucker!" he snapped.

Coughing and trying to catch her breath, Teagan grabbed the gun off the ground and knocked him over the head.

"Ugh... hmmm." she moaned, trying to catch her breath.

Spider, Gregory, and Gage walked toward her as the guard on the ground groaned to himself.

"Where's Kelton?" Teagan tilted her head and spat on the ground.

"He took off on a boat."

"Shit!"

She looked out to the water, seeing Kelton staring back at her.

"I need a boat."

"That can be arranged." Gage cocked his gun, nodding for them to follow over to the dock.

"Did all the girls get out?" Teagan ran toward the dock as Gage secured a boat.

"Yeah, Audrey and Neal are with the FBI now," Gregory said.

"They'll take credit for the arrest."

"It's better this way," Spider replied.

All three stepped on the boat, and Gage turned the ignition key as Gregory let the rope go from the dock.

"He has us beat by at least five minutes," Spider commented.

"Where do you think he's going?" Gage asked.

"He knows we're on to him; he can't get far," Teagan said.

Pushing the speed, Gage took off, trying to catch up to the boat carrying Todd.

"I see him up ahead." Gregory pointed at the boat.

"Get me close," Teagan said, removing her vest, standing close to the edge.

"What are you planning to do?"

"Whatever it takes," she responded.

"Copy that," Gage said.

"Hurry up! They're getting close." They heard Todd

shouting.

"Come on, a few more feet."

"Stop! This is the police," Gage yelled over the mic.

Todd pushed his driver off the boat, took the handle of the speed boat, and sped back up.

"Shit! That idiot." Gage spat.

Teagan lifted her gun, closing one eye, and stared at Todd's back, sending a shot toward his shoulder, causing him to cry out in pain and fall out of the boat. She passed the gun over to Spider and jumped in the water, swimming to pull Todd up before he drowned.

"Aghhh... help me... please," Todd cried out.

Grabbing him around the neck, she swam over to the boat and held him up as Gregory lifted him up by his shoulders. She pushed from the bottom, climbing in next. Steering the boat to the right, he went back to the dock. Teagan pulled the zip ties from her pockets, tying Todd by the wrists and ankles.

"I'm shot, I need a doctor," Todd groaned in pain.

"You'll get a doctor. When I think you deserve one."

The helicopters hovered above, and more police cars showed up as the boat finally arrived back. Hopping out of the boat, Teagan watched as Spider and Gregory helped Todd get out, and the EMTs loaded him on the stretcher.

"Agent Stone, we have all the girls accounted for and are checking with Homeland now," a police officer said.

"Wait a minute; I'm the secretary of transportation. Do you know what you're doing?" Todd complained, trying to remove the oxygen mask.

"The president is on the line." Daughtrey jogged over to her as she listened to news reporters calling out toward them.

"Mr. President?"

"You have him?" Sanders questioned.

"Yes, sir."

"I want him brought back to the White House," Sanders said.

"Mr. President, that might not be the wisest decision." Teagan ran a hand through her wet hair.

"What do you suggest?"

"We can't have a secretary from your cabinet show up after being captured."

"This is bad for my administration. I want him dealt with now," Sanders demanded and ended the call.

TODD KELTON RECEIVED medical help and got patched up by the ambulance. Teagan directed the team to take him once he was sedated to a safe house where they could talk with him. The room was built underground by the DC agency that Gage ran with his team. She asked everyone to leave the room while she spoke with him alone. Todd was tied up by his hands to the chair with grey tape over his mouth. Running her fingers over the tray of knives, Teagan listened as the cries got louder and louder. Smirking to herself, she picked up the army knife, turned around, and went to sit on the opposite side of the table from Kelton.

"Secretary Kelton, we finally meet."

He shook his head, crying and trying to move, but the rope was too tight, cutting off his circulation.

"I'm going to take the tape off, and you're going to answer my questions."

Standing up, she walked to him, scratching the knife against the table. She yanked the tape from his mouth.

"Ahhh!"

"Shhh... Sssh."

Teagan held the knife to her lips.

"Please, I didn't do anything."

"Mr. Kelton, please don't insult my intelligence."

"I can help you."

"Is this your way of trying to convince me to let you go?"

"I promise I can help."

"No, I doubt that, but what you've done is kill innocent girls."

"They're not girls!"

"Sick bastard." Teagan threw the knife into his shoulder, where he was shot.

"Bitch! Ughh... my shoulder."

"This is for those girls, you bastard." Teagan grabbed another knife from the tray, pulled Todd's head back, and slit his throat, dropping the blade on the ground. The doors opened, and Spider and Gregory checked Todd's pulse.

"What do you want the press release to say?" Gregory asked, picking up the knife from the floor.

"Make it a suicide; I don't care," Teagan answered, strolling out of the room and heading toward the entrance of the Agency. Seeing the cars ready to take them back, Teagan extended a hand for a shake.

"Is he dead?" Gage asked.

Holding the door open, Teagan nodded in answer.

"He won't be a problem any longer, and the president will replace his seat."

"I still can't believe he killed all those girls."

"I've seen worse, unfortunately," Teagan replied, sliding in her seat as Spider and Gregory came out a few minutes behind her, hopping in the front seats.

"See you next time, Agent Stone," Gage blurted out, tapping the hood of the Range Rover.

FIFTEEN

The next day.

Teagan woke up in bed, stretched her arms after feeling around the bed, checking for Christian. The flight came in late after she had a meeting with the president.

Flashback.

"How many girls did he kill?" the president asked again.

Gregory, Spider, and Teagan all glanced at each other as they sat in the Oval Office. It was past midnight, and he called them on the way to the airport to speak with them about Todd Kelton. It was running all over cable news about another scandal in the Sanders administration. Teagan stood in a jogging suit and tennis shoes that the president provided for them to change into when they arrived.

"From what we know so far, it could be over a dozen."

"Damn it, Stone."

President Sanders stood in front of the window, looking out at the moon.

"What about Steinman?"

"She's going to be investigated," Teagan said.

President Sanders pulled his chair out and sat, glancing at all three soldiers.

"Send all the parents my condolences," Sanders said.

"We will, sir," Spider said.

"Anything else I need to know?" Sanders questioned.

"It was clean."

PRESENT DAY.

Rising out of bed, Teagan grabbed the remote control and turned on the TV to the local news as breaking news spoke on Secretary Kelton's suicide and would give no further commit. President Sanders sent a statement through his press secretary.

"The president would like to send his condolences to Kelton's wife and children."

Teagan stood at the counter, brushing her teeth and placing her hair in a bun before she headed to the shower. She let the water rinse away the day before. Thirty minutes later, she sauntered in the kitchen smiling at her kids, laughing and talking while eating breakfast.

"Mommy, come eat breakfast," Tatum said.

"Mmmmm... smells good."

"I helped Daddy cook," Tatum said.

Teagan grabbed a plate from the counter, placing sausage, pancakes, and eggs on her plate.

"What are you three doing up on a weekend day?"

"I have a game today," CJ said.

"I want to go to the mall," Tatum said.

"A busy day, I see." Teagan kissed Cole on the cheek.

"We can go to the mall tomorrow, Tatum. Today's about your brother," Christian said.

"Boring," Tatum muttered.

"See, Mom, I told you to have another boy," CJ joked, pouring syrup on his pancakes.

"How about we go to your game, then go to the mall with just the two of us?" Teagan suggested.

"I like that idea better," Tatum responded, smiling with her missing right corner tooth.

"How long are you home, Mom?" CJ questioned.

"Officially on vacation, honey."

"Yes!" CJ raised his hand in the air for a high five.

Cole danced in his seat as everyone laughed at him.

"MOMMY, I LIKE THIS COLOR." Tatum held a pink crop top. This was the third store they'd visited, and Teagan was exhausted running behind Tatum after coming from a football game that CJ's team won. All she wanted to do was soak in a tub and sleep the rest of the day away, but Tatum had to try every store she saw. Holding four bags with mostly clothes for her daughter and one or two items she picked up for the boys, she wanted to spoil Tatum since she'd been away from her for so long.

"You're not wearing that, Tatum; try this instead." Teagan grabbed a long pink and blue jumpsuit with a sweater to match. Tatum rolled her eyes, and Teagan cocked her head to the side, passing the jumpsuit over for her to try on.

"Go ahead, try it on, and then we'll get our nails done." Teagan went to sit down on the bench as Tatum stepped into the dressing room.

"Do you need any help?" Teagan called out.

"No, I'm a big girl, Mommy."

Teagan lifted her cell phone out of her purse, checking in with Christian and the boys.

Teagan: Did you order pizza for dinner?"

Christian: Yep, along with hot wings.

Teagan: I might grab some movies.

Christian: Hurry home.

"Here I am." Tatum placed her hand on her hip.

"Oh, you look beautiful, baby." Teagan took a photo of Tatum, sending it to Christian

Teagan: Look at our baby.

Christian: Growing up too fast.

"I'll need shoes to match," Tatum informed her.

"You're just a little negotiator, aren't you?"

"I learned from you, Mommy." Tatum skipped back into the dressing room and changed. Teagan took the clothes she was holding and strolled toward the register to pay. Taking the receipt, Teagan passed the bag over to Tatum and left the store.

"Are we going to get our nails done?"

Tatum put on her seatbelt, taking her cell phone out to text with her friends.

"Who are you texting?"

"My friends."

"What friends?"

"I have friends."

"Do I know these friends?"

"Can I get colors on my nails this time?"

"No, you're not old enough for all that."

"Everyone does it, Mommy."

"Stop trying to grow up so fast."

Driving out of the parking structure, Teagan stopped at

the stop sign, waiting for the cars to turn before she got into traffic.

"Can we just go home?"

Tatum huffed, throwing her phone in her purse, sitting back with her arms crossed.

"Throwing a tantrum won't get you what you want, Tatum."

"Whatever."

Teagan was getting agitated at her daughter after the long day she had spoiled her. Arriving back home, Teagan parked, turning toward Tatum as she started to open the door to get out.

"Tatum, look at me."

She didn't move.

"Do you know how much you mean to me?" Teagan questioned.

"Yes," Tatum mumbled.

"Okay, so you know I would only do what's best for you."

"I know."

"You need to realize that your dad and I only want to protect you."

"Is that why you leave a lot for work?" she asked.

"Partially, yes, but you have to understand, you can't do everything like your friends."

"I get it, Mom."

"All right, let's go in and have pizza. Your dad wants to see your new clothes."

Teagan grabbed the bags as Tatum ran into the house, yelling for her brothers. Teagan shut the door behind her, putting the bags down on the ground. Walking up to Christian, she wrapped her arms around his waist, pecking him on the lips.

"How was shopping?" Christian inquired.

"Long."

He chuckled.

"She's stubborn like you." Christian tapped Teagan on the nose with his index finger.

"We've created a monster."

"Did you get cinnamon rolls too?"

"I did; I figured you forgot to ask when you texted, so I ordered a box with the wings."

"I could get used to this."

"To what?"

"Being a wife and mom."

"Are you saying you're retiring from The Firm?" Christian leaned his face back, staring at her.

"Considering how much we've been through over these last few years."

"Mom, come watch the movie," Cole asked.

"What did you order?"

"*The Conjuring*," Cole said.

Teagan jerked back in shock.

"He's going to be up all night with nightmares."

"That's fine; his mother will be here to read him a bedtime story."

Chuckling, she took a seat between Cole and CJ, taking some popcorn from the bowl and watching as the commercial previews came on. This was the time she enjoyed, when they could all be together and relax as a family without any worries—splurging on pizza, junk food, and movies.

"Glad you're back, babe." Christian lifted Tatum from the loveseat, letting her sit in his lap.

"Me too." Teagan winked her left eye, eating more popcorn.

SIXTEEN

One week later.

Teagan stood patiently in the corner, staring at the one-way mirror. Spider and the CIA director argued against having this meeting. Getting special permission from the president to allow an unorthodox questioning of a criminal after having the senate hearings might bring more eyes on The Firm. The door opened with a guard in front and behind Audrey while chained at the wrists and legs. The news was still running the story over the massive human trafficking crime that almost went down, and to know it was a woman at the helm made Teagan's skin crawl. Teagan turned around with her arms crossed over her chest, studying Audrey's demeanor.

"Can you give us some privacy?" Teagan asked.

"We were told to stay," the guard replied.

"I think I'll be fine, don't you think, Audrey?" Teagan cocked her head to the side.

"You'll be fine."

Both guards looked at each other, then nodded, heading

out of the room. Stepping forward, Teagan pulled the chair out and sat down, crossing her legs with her hands in her lap.

"Why?" Teagan asked.

Audrey smiled.

"Is this some type of *Law and Order* interrogation?"

"No, I just want to know why."

Audrey bent forward.

"I like money," Audrey answered.

"How long have you been doing this?"

"I'd rather not do the whole abused, manipulated thing."

"Then explain to me how you ended up here?"

"Agent Stone, it's simple—I'm a businesswoman."

"Selling girls?"

Audrey shrugged her shoulders.

"You have a cigarette?" Audrey asked.

"I don't smoke."

Staring at Teagan, Audrey looked behind her at the mirror.

"How many people are behind the mirror?"

"Enough."

"I don't have a sad, soppy story."

"I think you do; something changed for you to become this way."

"Please don't psychoanalyze me."

"Do you know you're going to jail for a very long time?"

"I had a good run."

"All of those families trusted you, and this is what you do."

"What do you want?"

"Give me all the names and information of any other people involved."

"What do I get?"

"You get to live."

Audrey ran a hand through her hair, blowing out a breath and taking a few minutes to stare into Teagan's eyes, wondering if she was serious.

"Fine."

"Thank you."

Teagan rose from her seat, walked to the door, and knocked for the guards to reenter.

CAMDEN, Nebraska

Stepping out of the car wearing her shades, Teagan brought a few men with her in case things got out of hand. Spider was across the street on the roof, zoned in on his target if they tried to take a shot. She was here to collect the final piece of the puzzle before moving on and giving all the families closure. Opening the door of the Camden police station, Bert stopped talking to Peter at the front desk as Teagan led the team of ten FBI agents inside.

"I need to see Chief Barrett."

"Why?" Bert questioned.

"Either you step aside, or we can do this the hard way."

"What is this about?" Peter asked.

"My friends here have a warrant for his arrest." Teagan pointed to the agent standing next to her.

"That's ridiculous," Bert blurted out.

"I don't have time to go back and forth with you, Bert."

"You've done enough to hurt our town. Just leave, bitch!" Bert barked.

Teagan smirked as she pushed through the door with the agents behind her.

"Call me a bitch again. I dare you," Teagan told him, cocking a left brow up.

Peter stepped between them.

"Just go do what you came to do," Peter said.

Glancing at Peter, then back at Bert, Teagan stepped around him and stalked toward Chief Barrett's office. Barging through his door, Teagan took the phone out of his hand.

"The chief will have to call you back in five to ten years." She hung up the phone.

"Hey!"

"Chief Barrett, you're under arrest."

"Are you crazy!" Chief Barrett jumped up, charging toward Teagan.

"I wouldn't do that, Chief."

An FBI agent pushed him back up against the wall.

"We know everything."

"I never touched those girls!"

"I never said anything about girls, Chief."

Chief Barrett started sweating, looking nervous.

"I want a lawyer."

"Funny, you're asking for help when I bet you didn't try to help those girls."

I HOPE you enjoyed Teagan's story so far. Please also check out "**Agent Red (Death) Teagan Stone Book 6" here** https://authoravasking.squarespace.com/agent-red-book-6 with a host of characters intertwined. Also, if you love Mystery, Suspense check out free prequel **Mirror of Lies Book 1" here** https://payhip.com/b/XoQ7.

Check out free short here: ***"The Firm"*** https://payhip.com/b/py7S

Grab Boxset "**Agent Red 1-3**" here https://payhip.com/b/1KcxY

AGENT RED:FATAL DEATH (TEAGAN STONE BOOK6)

Teagan Stone has walked a fine line between life and death. This time she's come across an enemy that doesn't care if she's the most trained killer or not. They only want one thing, and that's to see Agent Red brought to her knees. In a race against time, she will have to make the ultimate decision. Will she be able to save someone close to her or put the country she gave the oath to protect before her happiness?

MIRROR OF LIES BOOK 1

Alison and Jessica were the best of friends of middle and high school. Fifteen years later, Jessica, now an up-and-coming journalist, learns that Alison has been killed in a car accident. But that's not the most troubling part of this tragedy.

Alison died with a secret that only she, Jessica, and a small group of friends know. Her fear is that secret didn't die with her friend.

If it didn't, what does that mean for her and the others who know what happened all those years ago?

READING ORDER OF SERIES

Agent Red-Fatal Memory Book 1
https://books2read.com/u/4j2PYX
Agent Red-Fatal Target Book 2
https://books2read.com/u/bWP8Jq
Agent Red-Fatal Crime Book 3
https://books2read.com/u/mZadZJ
Agent Red-Fatal Justice Book 4
https://books2read.com/u/mqo7wd
Agent Red-Fatal Enemy Book 5
https://books2read.com/u/bxeo1q
Agent Red-Fatal Death Book 6
Agent Red-Fatal Revenge Book 7
Agent Red-Fatal Pursuit Book 8
Agent Red-Fatal Attack Book 9
Agent Red-Fatal Mission Book 10

ACKNOWLEDGMENTS

I want to thank my team, who helps me behind the scenes, from my editors to my test readers and graphic designers, and the list goes on. I truly appreciate each of you for keeping me on my toes.

ABOUT THE AUTHOR

Ava S. King writes mystery, psychological crime thrillers, international espionage thrillers, political and action/adventure novels. Her debut novel, Agent Red Fatal Memory became a huge hit with 100 BestSellers, Top Indie Favorite. 100 Debut release on all digital platforms. Born and raised in TN, filmmaker and lover of all things mystery and suspense. In addition to writing, Ava loves bringing her novels to life on the bigscreen starting with Agent Red series.

If you want to know when the next book will come out, please visit my website at http://www.authoravasking.com, where you can sign up to receive an email for her next release.

WHAT'S NEXT?

Want to know what happens next? Follow me at the links below to catch the next release.

Thank you so much for reading, and if you enjoyed the crazy ride and decided to leave a review, we'd truly appreciate the support. Reviews are the lifeblood of the publishing world. They're read, appreciated, and needed. Please consider taking the time to leave a few words on Goodreads or BookBub.

Sign up for updates and sneak peeks at the sites below:
www.authoravasking.com

304 PUBLISHING COMPANY

We showcase authors writing African American, Interracial, Women's Fiction, Romance, Erotic, Thriller, Suspense. Plus, Mystery, Poetry, Beauty, and Style Books. Join our mailing list to stay updated with new releases and blog posts.